Women o...
Adventure w...

By
Carol Sumilas Boshears

Keith Publications, LLC
www.keithpublications.com
©2016

Arizona
USA

To Donna,
forever my
AMC friend,
Carol S. Boshears

Women on Fire
Adventure with Flair

Copyright© 2016

By Carol Sumilas Boshears

Edited by Vanessa Gothreau
nessa8169@hotmail.com

Proofread by Betty Gelean
Bgelean@xplornet.ca

Cover art by Cristian Aluas

Cover art Keith Publications, LLC © 2016
www.keithpublications.com

ISBN: 978-1-62882-139-0

If you are interested in purchasing more works of this nature, please stop by
www.keithpublications.com

Contact information: keithpublications@cox.net
Visit us at: www.keithpublications.com

Printed in The United States of America

Reviews

I loved Women on Fire. It was riveting. The book did a great job of presenting well rounded, fully developed characters - by the end the reader feels like they actually KNOW these people. The plot was engaging and my only complaint is I wanted more. Sequel please.

> Chief Executive Officer Private Public Solutions
> Theresa Bulger

Egypt is keen to leave her family and the small town where they live to seek a life of her own. She has studied Egyptian

artefacts and wants to find a job, which will take her well away from the family firm. Therefore, when she is offered a position with a company dealing in antiquities, she can't believe her luck. However, as the weeks pass, Egypt finds that all is not as it seems and she and her best friend, Gina begin to investigate.

I found this to be a light-hearted mystery, with a touch of humor. Egypt's search for the truth takes the reader down several blind alleys before finally disclosing the real reason why she was hired for the job. They were times when I smiled at Egypt and Gina's exploits, especially their shopping expeditions. But there were moments when I held my breath, as the plot began to unfold and the two friends found themselves in trouble. This is a good read, a story you won't want to put down until the very end.

-Eileen Thorton, author of The Trojan Project, Divorcees.Biz and Twelve Days

Dedication

To my husband, Jim, who said, "I think you have something here."

Acknowledgements

A special thank you to Anita Burns for her help and editing knowledge, and Mark Terence Chapman for telling me not to give up. And to my special Keith Publications editor, Vanessa Gothreau.

T is for Trouble

The dim and gritty room smelled like dust and mold. The rusty iron-framed bed was flanked by a couple of creaky wooden chairs. In the corner was a not-so-clean toilet in a tiny open room. Gina looked out the dirt laden tiny window that had rusted iron bars. Vodka bottles were strewn across the floor.

Against my better judgment, I sat cross-legged near a stained cot, hoping there weren't any crawly creatures hiding in the torn ticking. I trembled with frustration. No, I didn't mean for it to turn out like this. I'm such a damn fool. It's my fault. Now, my wild schemes might get us killed.

"Look, Egypt, you didn't drag me screaming into this. I came seeking answers, too. I wanted this as much as you. So, shut up, already. Let's show the courage we've always had. Remember saving Luigi from those Albanians in Italy? That took guts and courage."

Biting my lower lip, I knew she was right. Still, I was worried. "Sure. Until now, I had courage. This is the Russian mob we're dealing with. Mobs like this can be brutal, especially Russian mobs. It begins with being tied to a pole, and after that, only God knows what." I pressed my hands to my temples to stop the throbbing. "What the hell was I thinking? How could I have come up with this mindless plan in the first place? This is a disaster."

Gina stared at me with that squinty-eyed look that I knew meant she was using anger to cover her fear. I was sure she thought I'd given up. I squared my shoulders and returned her gaze. "Well?"
"Okay, Egypt. Let's stop this crap and evaluate our possibilities—like you taught me. You're the genius here, so stop whining and put that twisted brain of yours in gear. This should be a slam-dunk for you."

"We were ambushed. It happened so fast, I couldn't think." I lowered my voice to a whisper. "Don't glower at me like that. I'm not a miracle-worker."

I regretted the insane decision to uncover the real story about the mix-up with the drugs, but concealed it from Gina. She was already overwrought. Instead I surveyed our surroundings and sized-up our captors. I knew we had to escape soon. This was no time for fear and hesitation. I had to think and think fast. Taking a deep breath I closed my eyes. Images of what happened began unfolding in my inner vision. *How do we get out of this?*

After a few minutes, I opened my eyes. My solutions came up as empty as a wino's bottle. *How did I think we were so invincible that we could accomplish anything? What a fool.*

My hands shook and my stomach twisted into tight knots. I was scared. We both knew that we had to be gone before Kostya arrived. He's not called "The Bull" for nothing. This could mean painful deaths.

Shock waves traveled down my spine and then up to my head. I shivered. "Gina, I have nothing at the moment. I don't know what to do. Give me time." It was a necessity to show her promise.

"Well, I guess we just wait to find out what the mob decides." I sat hunched over hugging my knees. Tears threatened. Then a flash burst into my brain.

"Gina! Something we should have remembered. It was your idea."

"What are you babbling about, Egypt?"

"Our boots, Gina, our boots!" I lowered my voice so the guards couldn't hear. "How stupid can we be? We have to try. How can you forget again?"

CHAPTER ONE

When I first started looking for a job with my eye on New York City, my main motivation was to get out of my stifling home town. My never-cut-the-cord Mom is loopy. I felt smothered by her constant pressure to go into the family business. Really, I have absolutely no interest in stuffing sausages at our Polish deli. I needed to run, and fast, before it was too late to get away.

My best friend, Gina was the only one I confided in when I started scoping out prospective jobs. It was fun, like a top secret military exercise. She had a controlling, smothering family too, and was fed up with "Tinyville," so I persuaded her to hop on the adventure train with me.

"Well, Gina, are you ready to help me get out of here and be my rock?"

"Sure am. Maybe it will give me the guts to move on. I'll be your rock—you can be my experiment. If it works out for you, I might just pull up stakes and join you permanently."

"Cripes, your experiment? Thanks pal, now I feel like a lab rat," I laughed. "Really though, I'm glad to do it. I'll take the first step but only if you promise to make one too, and soon. I have a bit of money saved from my last crummy job."

"You got it, Egypt. With everything that's in me, I promise to get the hell out of this place. You know I want to. You know we needn't worry about resources either."
"I know that, but I hesitate to ask and take advantage of your friendship."

I believed her but soon discovered that I had one more hurdle. A few days after our talk about escaping, Gina called me. "I had a blowout with my family. I told them I was leaving. They threw everything at me!" she cried into the phone. "They pounded me with their argument that family is more important than some stupid adventure and fast cars, and why couldn't I be more frugal with the money Uncle Tony left me. They just kept bullying me."

She blustered on for fifteen minutes before winding down and moving past hurt into anger. "I'm pissed. Still, better to be pissed off than on, I guess." She laughed.

"Gina, calm yourself. You'll figure it out."

"Damn. Who cares? I'm old enough to make my own decisions—good or bad. Screw them. I'm ready to hustle out of here!"

"Great!"

So we plotted our escape. Gina's family was all about loyalty and obligation. My family, well, Mom was controlling and smothering. She never understood my desire to work in the field of antiquities. Which is odd, since she also loved ancient history and antiques. She adored auctions. That's where I learned all about antiques. But to her, that was an "interest," a hobby, not something to make a living at. She knew I was enthralled with the ancient world. It was mesmerizing and virtually placed me in a trance at times. I admit that my mother would let me know of any TV event involving the ancient world was coming on. Rome enthralled me almost as much as Egypt. But it is what it is.

The family business. Now, in my mother's mind, that was a real job. With me she is not as persuasive as she thinks, even with a meat cleaver in her hand. Her preoccupation with grinding sausage drove me crazy. And her 'magnificent' obsession about her holy visions of Jesus and Mary in strange places and objects is beyond disturbing.

I was thinking that my grandpa, with whom I am close, would support my decision. He was one hell of a man, and one of vision, despite his age. I heard once that in his youth he tore a phonebook in two. Oh, it wasn't to show his strength, mind you. It was because the phone company forgot to place his store's big ad in their book. He made the threat in front of them too! Now that's nothing to fool around with. He can grind that kielbasa until it squeals.

When I think back to the day Gina and I left home, I have to laugh. We had planned so carefully. I timed it so that Mom was occupied at the far end of the house. I tried to leave on the sly. But, when I padded across the hallway, Mom spotted me.

"Egypt Ann Isis Briggs. Where do you think you're going? You promised your Aunt Nellie you would help her at the shop this afternoon."

There she stood, blocking my way. She was a huge boulder in the road to freedom. Her face flushed with anger, eyes like a hungry hawk. I had to think quickly, "Uh, no, Mom. That's tomorrow. Gina and I are going shopping and then we're having a late dinner with friends."

She gave me the evil eye. "Tomorrow? You'd better not have that mixed up. You know how Aunt Nellie can be."

I smiled then whispered under my breath. "Yeah, it runs in the family."

"Say, what?"

"Nothing, Mom. I have it right. Ask her if you don't believe me."

She relaxed her stance a little and took a deep breath. I could tell she was preparing some snarky comeback.

3

"Okay. Go on, be with your friends. While you're out wasting your time, I'm doing important work." She turned and stomped off, shaking her head and mumbling under her breath.

While she considered my time being wasted, her making rosaries was important.

She wiled away her "spare" time making rosaries. She gave one to everyone she came in contact with, even those of the Jewish persuasion. Her comment was, "Go ahead, and take them. Say your own prayers. Think of it as God's universal prayer wheel. He won't mind." Though reluctant, they accepted with grace.

"I'll be late. Gina and I are having that dinner with our friends. Bye."

So, I met Gina at the end of my street where my suitcases were safely and secretly ensconced in her car.

"Time to scoot," she said and revved her Porsche as I settled my lying ass into the seat. Off to New York we went, full of hope that it would be everything we envisioned. I tried not showing her how scared I was. I reiterated to her, "Our world has been small, Gina. We have to "spelunk" the world and its many corners, spooky or not. My parents, on the other hand, want me grinding sausage! And I refuse to do that." I think the word spelunk lost her.

Inside I was shaking at the prospect of going, even with my best friend. Looking back, I feel a bit silly for being so scared.

Gina and I moved into a small apartment. I faced the music and called my mom. She wasn't happy about me moving out on my own, and especially not happy about how I did it. A tearful half-hour later, all was forgiven. Naturally, she had to tell Aunt Nellie too.

4

Gina had a similar show-down with her family. At first, they threatened her with several disturbing scenarios like making her a family outcast. However, being Italian she knew family was too important and it would never happen. By the time they had finished bickering, all was well. Her accounts were intact and poised to use any way she wanted. And for her, the top of her list was shopping. As her departed Uncle Tony's favorite, she reaped his rewards.

She had more money than she could ever count, but wanted to do something interesting. She found part time work at a florist and put her considerable artistic eye to good use.

It wasn't long before I found an ad for a company called Eternal Treasures. They were looking to hire someone in research regarding antiquities. It sounded perfect for me. Even though I didn't have any actual field experience, I had studied ancient languages and I had a degree in archaeology. Plus, I did a lot of independent study on antiquities of the ancient world.

The job might involve travel, too. I prayed that if I was hired, I would one day be sent to my namesake, Egypt. That would be the pinnacle of all I desired.

As I was walking in for my interview appointment, my confidence wavered slightly. I had never applied to a company as large and successful as this one—and in New York to boot. Gina's words echoed in my brain. *"For heaven's sake, will you stop fidgeting? You're making me nervous. It's not like its Judgment Day and God is in New York to size you up."*

Still, I felt like I was in Hades, already. This was a juncture in my life, the first of its kind.

As I sat in the reception area at Eternal Treasures, every fiber of my being screamed that this would be my dream job. *They have to hire me. They just have to.*

***

I was apprehensive. After being told to wait, which seemed like an eternity to me—I was called into the inner office. A middle-aged woman sat behind an immaculately clean desk. Her hair was pulled back so tight into a bun it made her face look like a bad cosmetic surgery job.

She studied my application, making some notes in the margins.

"Hmmm. I see your qualifications are good. . ."
This was hopeful.

"Good. I see you speak some Arabic."

She scribbled a note. "I see. I see. You have a variety of skills. Mr. Hill will like that." She closed her notebook and stood, extending her hand toward a door. "Follow me, please."

My stomach churned and a morsel of sweat slid down my back.

'Bun Babe' as I christened her, opened the door and was beckoning me to wait.

I gulped. Simply looking at the door gave me the crypt-creeps. I heard her talking to who I found out afterwards, was Mr. Bruce Hill. I shifted so I could see them through the partially open door.

"I have someone interesting you might like for the *special* position."

Mr. Hill leaned back in his enormous chair, Mont Blanc pen in hand.

"Her qualifications are impressive—a degree in archaeology and a good education in antiquities, plus she speaks a little Arabic."

He looked up and drummed the desk with his fingers. "It seems she has it covered." He lowered his voice to a whisper. "Hmmm. Nice. She could be the one we've been looking for."

Bun Babe came to the door and gestured for me to go in. I heard the door click as she left.

He waved me closer. "Have a seat, Egypt, excuse me, Ms. Briggs."

I was so nervous; I tripped and nearly fell on my face. I felt like such a klutz, I wanted to run away and hide. I sat in one of the leather chairs in front of his desk. "Egypt is fine."

"Just a moment." He busied himself looking for something.

I glanced around. The desk was definitely Louis XVI, mahogany, tastefully adorned with gold. The Impressionist artwork was beautiful and worth a small fortune.

A call came in. He looked at me apologetically and answered it. I had a moment to study him. Handsome, beautiful build, deep blue eyes and jet black hair, tousled just enough.

Disconnecting the call, he stared at me. After going over my qualifications and asking some personal questions about my interest in antiquities, he abruptly asked, "Is your passport in order?"

My heart skipped a beat. Travel would be awesome! I didn't tell him how much I hated flying. Well, it's more like terror than hate. I sucked it up. "It is, sir."

He went on to tell me some of my duties—attending auctions, researching, dealing with difficult situations regarding antiquities…. My mind was so full I didn't hear much more than that—except that I would start on Monday. Holy crap! I was in. "Thank you, Mr. Hill."
"Call me Bruce."

"At first your salary won't be as much as it should be; however, we own great inexpensive apartments where you can live. I hope $50,000 for a start will be agreeable with you."

Almost choking, I wavered a touch and trying to sound cool, replied, "Yes, that is favorable with me."
Then I nervously babbled on about his choice in art and decor before I noticed he wasn't paying attention any longer. The meeting was over. He touched the intercom.

"Yes, Mr. Hill?"

"Please fill Egypt in on job duties, show her to her office, and give her information about the apartments in the building for rent."

"Yes, sir. I'll also have her fill out the proper papers." The intercom went silent.

I turned to leave. As I neared the door a man rushed in, nearly knocking me over. Bruce called out, "Trevor, come in. I'd like you to meet our newest addition. Egypt, this is Trevor. I'm thinking she'll give us the push we need."

And, I thought *Bruce* was gorgeous. Trevor had him beat hands down.

"Welcome to our little family, Egypt."
He also offered me what I discovered was the deal of the century, in my living situation. "Ms. Briggs, there are

apartments in this building we own. We could rent one to you for a nominal fee. But I'm sure Bruce must have told you?" He mentioned a paltry sum.

If the apartment was anything like his office it couldn't be too shabby.

I must have blushed hot pink as I rushed out the door.

***

It wasn't until I hit the street that I could breathe again. I could hardly believe it. I got the job! When I met Gina for lunch, I talked a lot about Trevor. "Tall, perfect body, oval face and deep dark-brown hair. Did I mention his adorable aquiline nose! Oh, and heavenly blue eyes that gleam of let's have some fun."

"Sounds like he'd be a perfect match for a tall blue-eyed blonde I know."

CHAPTER TWO

It was late and my neck hurt. After a week, I was beginning to think this job wasn't going to be the adventure I'd hoped for.

The air conditioning was on the blink and the fan next to my desk only seemed to blow the heat around. I flipped through web pages looking for information on an antique vase slated for auction. Nothing.

My sweaty, slippery fingers rolled down the keyboard like a pianist on the wrong keys, and a file I'd never seen before loaded. I'm sure this information must have been accidentally left unlocked. I doubt that I was supposed to have access as it appeared quite unusual.

Intrigued, I leaned in closer to the screen. *These letters are really odd. They don't make sense. Maybe hieroglyphs? Hmmm. Not Egyptian, though, I think. No, I know.*

I was so focused on these odd letters I forgot how hot it was in the room. *Well, I don't really believe in accidents. Somehow I was meant to see this.* I recalled the theory that the future happens seconds before it really does. Something about a signal sent to our brains and *voilá*—the future is perceived after it happened.

Scrolling through the file, I thought it perplexing that Eternal Treasures would be dabbling in something like this. I think cryptic languages might be out of their area of expertise. However, I couldn't know for sure. It was connected to antiquities in some way though. Translations of ancient languages might be needed for some artifacts.

I know about hieroglyphs. Looking closer, I realized, however, that they weren't true hieroglyphs. *Arabic? No. These are actual Roman alphabet letters but turned in different ways and symbols of some kind.* I ran a finger down the screen. "And...they're arrows, slashes and odd diacritical marks."

I glanced at my door to make sure it was shut. I was certain this was a confidential file and probably access to it was restricted. I wasn't told that translating was a part of my job description anyway. There would be no reason for it I figured. My fingers tingled with excitement. *I do love mystery and intrigue!*

As my imagination cranked into full speed, I was already off on a new quest to find out what these letters were all about and why Eternal Treasures had them in a confidential file. I realized that in any adventure there are lots of questions and answers that don't come easily. They have to be hunted down like prey. My mind started running amok with vague and unlikely ideas.

If I take on this quest, I can't count on anyone at the company being forthcoming. People here seem so hush, hush. They don't seem to trust anyone. Their eyes reflect near constant worry and suspicion. Plus, they are always hurrying and scurrying. A peculiar lot. They recover antiquities to repatriate them, and auction valuable antiques. Why all the secrecy?

***

That night I told Gina about my discovery. "This is more odd than. . . I don't know what." I sighed. "It's so peculiar. I'd swear I was looking at an ancient language, or maybe a code. I don't remember anything in college that resembled this."

"You're going to do some digging, aren't you, Egypt?"

"Of course! Do you know anyone who might be able to help? I'd love to know what these letters or symbols mean. Don't you think it would be spectacular to decode it?"

Gina gave me that look, the one that said, 'I'm in, even if it's a wild goose chase. "You know I'll find a way to participate," she replied with assurance. "I'm excited for you."

"I feel refueled and on fire." I felt the burning way deep in my heart, and the pit of my stomach. "I feel jacked up like a Super Sport, like you and I were years ago." We missed that anticipation of excitement. This was going to be fascinating. "I'm exhilarated."

She sat hand-on-chin as if in deep thought. "My cousin Vince graduated from Princeton. He's a whiz at everything and he knows everyone who's anyone." She sat up straighter and took in a deep breath. "Egypt, wait. What about *your* cousin?"

I perked up. "Yes! I'd forgotten about nerdy Reggie. He might be able to help. He knows all the geeks." I laughed. "They even have an annual Greatest Geek Contest. One year, the prizes were a pencil box and a slide rule." Slapping my palms on the table, I blurted, "We'll get to the bottom of what's going on if it takes Atlas to pry it out."

A crazy notion hit me. *My company's name is Eternal Treasures—E.T. Oh, heavens. Would the odd letters have something to do with E.T.s? Stop it Egypt. You're letting your imagination run away with you.* I dropped the notion, yet E.T. echoed in my head.

I turned my thoughts to Eternal Treasures. It was an interesting company with a variety of functions—maybe too many. In my opinion, they spread themselves pretty thin, but as smooth as peanut butter. I had noticed that they were having problems with a rival company, Crypto. . .something.

I vowed to keep my eyes and ears open. *I don't want to be Mary going to the well and finding it dry!*

"You know what, Gina? Eternal Treasures is having some sort of problem with another company. Maybe they're trying to waylay us for vindication or some sort of prize?"

"Sounds plausible. You know what that means don't you?" She rubbed her hands together as if she was ready to take on a spy mission.
"Sure do. I think we're in trouble, girl." I knew we were. I felt it in the pit of my stomach. My premonitions always meant trouble.

***

The next day, I was staring at my computer monitor, studying my discovery and puzzling over it. After growing even more confused, I resolved to march into Bruce's office and ask him about it. After all, maybe he meant for me to see it but hasn't yet told me.

Closing my office door behind me, I stepped quietly toward Bruce's office. As I neared, I heard my name. Someone was talking about me. By the sound of it, the other person was Trevor. I stopped just outside the door that was open by a crack.

"I think Egypt will work out fine. She knows her business and doesn't mind going to auctions. Plus, she probably won't ask too many questions." Bruce lowered his voice. "We'll do California when the time is right. That'll be easy. Our contacts there need the info we just gathered."

"You're sure it's hidden inside the slip of the vase?" asked Trevor. "We have to be careful. If Cryptonomics finds out, we could be in trouble."

Bruce was silent for a moment. "Crypto is doing everything it can to beat us to the punch. It's good they're in the dark about how much we know about them. I just hope they're the fools we think they are. As long as they're stupid enough to follow us, we'll be fine."

I heard the familiar sound of a microwave door and the aroma of popcorn wafted through the door. Trevor's deep voice came loud and clear. "As long as our reputation for being pillars of truth goes untarnished, no one will doubt our motives or our word. Here have some."

I made out the sound of typing on a keyboard and the click of a mouse.

"Ah, here's the report. We should get to work on funding. Our men in Egypt think thirty million dollars isn't nearly enough."

I pulled back when I heard Trevor sigh and head for the door. But the footsteps moved away again.

Pacing?

"I agree. We've been working on this for a long time. We're finally close. If it takes fifty million or more, it's worth it."

"I'm worried that Crypto is also getting close," said Bruce. A blip sounded as if he had closed a file on his computer. "Our intel reports that Crypto has someone who can translate the ancient script. We have to move fast before they discover the location of the burial chamber. We need to protect it at any cost, even with lives if necessary."

A chair creaked and the footsteps stopped. "Well," said Trevor, "we have vital information they don't. While we're closing in on the prize, they'll be hauling tons of sand out of the wrong place. They'll come up empty-handed. Hopefully, by that time, we will have retrieved the device."

"Yes," said Bruce. "They're stupid, greedy, and power hungry—no match for our network."
I froze on the spot. Was the file I discovered what they were talking about? I knew I should turn on my heels, get back to my office and keep my knowledge of this very, very secret.

Once back in my office, I took screen shots of the file, printed them out and folded them into my purse. I went back to the antique candelabra I was supposed to be researching for an auction. My hands shook. *What did I get myself into?* It was both terrifying and exciting.

CHAPTER THREE

A few days later, Trevor told me, "After lunch I'll be showing you your new apartment," he continued on in his Head of the Welcome Committee role. "Just come to my office."

Boy, lucky the old, small as a closet, place I had was a month to month rental.

His eyes, those eyes. Deep, deep pools of pure sexiness—that's what they were. I thought of him often. And boy, did he have a great butt too.

This new home is also an adventure for me. I never thought I'd live in luxury. All the furniture I needed or wanted flew out like a vision. The rest rounded out the main living space's decor. Then we moved on to the bedroom. Delectable was the word. A cross between Art Deco and transitional, my trained antique eye noted. The apartment even boasted a spare bedroom.

When I made my way into the bathroom, my heels clicked on the tile floor—that natural stuff, you know. There was an endless supply of linens and such filling the shelves and cabinets.

But the best feature was the Jacuzzi tub!

I cast a seductive glance at Trevor and thought, *my adventure just got more interesting.*

Two weeks into my job, Gina and I settled into our new apartment. Yes, ours, in the Eternal Treasures building. It was truly magnificent with all its features and antique replicas. I flopped across the king-sized bed to think about my life so far. Outside, the soothing sound of rain on the grey streets below cleared my head. *Sunday or no Sunday, I'm not going anywhere today.*

The delicious secret of the mystery thrilled me. I took the printed files of the strange letters out of my purse. Adventure. I loved every second of it. I was a new person in New York. But I couldn't hold a candle to Gina's transformation. To her, this city was a veritable smorgasbord, and it was her fashionista dream.
I heard the front door open.

"Egypt? Are you here?"

"In my room," I called out.

She swooped in and threw a multitude of bags stuffed with what I assumed were amazing clothes on my bed. I already had noticed a collection of bags in her room. She was a bit droopy from the rain, but nonetheless upbeat.

"Do you really go to the garment district to get "firsts" or do you just like to have bragging rights for knowing all the "in" people?"
She twirled around in an exquisite skirt from one of the latest up-and-coming New York designers. "Well, yes, Miss Know-It-All. I *do* know some people but that's not my main reason for going."

I wondered then what her reason was. Shaking my head, I could think only that the garment district must love her. Gina dressed like royalty and wouldn't be caught dead without her just short of long hair perfectly styled. There were times when I envied the loads of dough she had inherited. I sometimes called her the Bank of Gina. But for the sake of our friendship, I never asked for favors regarding money. I paid my half of the rent and utilities even though to her it would have been pocket change to foot the complete bill.

Gina had originally agreed to come with me to New York with slight reservations about staying, but I had an inkling she was here for good.

"Honey," said Gina, glancing at the papers on the bed, "I'm curious. Well, to be honest, I'm nosey."

"Yes, and?" I grinned. "Like I don't know that? You're busting to solve this mystery as much as I am."

She lifted her chin. "So what? I'm Italian. Italians love to buck the system. You know I'll go nearly anywhere if fun is to be had."

"And," I added, "If it entails defying the rules, you'll jump at the chance. That's one of the reasons we've been best friends since we were children."

"True," said Gina looking at me with those beautiful root beer eyes coupled with a brazen take-on-the-world look that defied her tiny stature. "And the shopping is amazing here—almost as good as in Paris." She laughed.

"So true." I knew she was there for me. If I wanted to go to the moon, she would find a way to make it happen—for both of us.
As if reading my mind, her face softened and she wrapped her arms around me in a hug. "I got your back, honey. Never despair. It's Gina in charge."

"I know. I never doubted." *Dear me, I questioned, Gina in charge? Sure, I'd like to see that day.*

She stepped back and smoothed her skirt. "Well, ready to go?"

"Go?"

"To dinner, silly."

"Oh! Uh, sure. There went my day of chillin'.

CHAPTER FOUR

I stretched and yawned, turning over in my super-king bed and designer sheets. I loved my apartment. I climbed out of bed and opened the curtains. The early fall air drifted in. Cool, crisp, but warm at the same time. I inhaled the leaves veiled in majestic colors. It was wonderful. *Maybe I'll drive to New England and gaze at the trees. Mmmmm.*

"Hey, girl,"

I turned. It was Gina standing in the doorway.

"Hey, yourself. Come in."

She ambled into the room. It's such a beautiful day. Let's go shopping!"

"I sort of wanted to spend Sunday driving to New England to look at the autumn leaves, but shopping afterwards sounds great."

"Wonderful." She grinned and danced out. "See you in a few."

I went into the bathroom and turned on the shower. *Tomorrow I'm going to get to the bottom of what Bruce and Trevor were talking about.* A voice in the back of my head echoed, *be careful.*

***

Monday morning, I arrived at work early. I wanted to see if the mysterious file was still accessible from my computer. "Yesss." There it was, as strange as the first time I saw it.

People started to arrive so I clicked off the screen and pulled up my project for the day. I couldn't keep my mind on it, though. I needed to mingle with the others in the office to see if I could glean any clues about what in the hell is going on around here.

The click clack of my stiletto heels echoed heading toward the employee lounge, coffee cup in hand. When I rounded a corner, I almost slammed into a woman I hadn't seen before. She was a tall, dark-rooted blond with searing brown eyes that stared at me with what felt like X-ray vision.

"Oh! Excuse me," I said, backing away. She just stood there for a moment. I knew she was sizing up the new girl. "Hi, I'm Egypt." I extended a hand.

She hesitated a moment then clasped my fingers in a surprisingly strong grip. "I'm Sparrow, Assistant Vice President of Marketing."

I looked over her shoulder and froze. Coming our way was Trevor. *Damn. I know he and Bruce are up to something. Why does he have to be so gorgeous? Hard to think of him as sneaky and...not sure what.*

"Hello, Egypt," he said, flashing a perfect, mind-melting smile. "Settling in?"

I had a hard time tearing myself away from his amazing eyes. "Uh. Yes. Thanks. Everything's perfect." I regained some of my composure. "And, the apartment is great!"
He smiled again.

Oh, God. Focus, Egypt. "I'm nearly finished with the report on the Third Dynasty Egyptian Red Stone Vase."

Nodding, he moved to leave. "Great, just send it to me as soon as it's complete."

I watched his perfect behind walk away.

"Ahem." It was Sparrow. "Welcome aboard, Egypt. We'll be working closely together on your auction jaunts and assignments."

She pushed past me and disappeared into an office on the left.

Phew! My shoulders relaxed and I could breathe again. *Something about her scares me.*

***

That night, as I was sitting on a stool in my perfectly shiny ultra-modern kitchen, eating delivered pizza, something occurred to me. *Why would Eternal Treasures set me up in this amazing, expensively furnished apartment? I wasn't top management. Then there is the cryptic file I discovered.*

I jumped as my cell buzzed on the countertop. It was Gina. "Hey girl. What's up?"

"Thought you might like a night out. There's a new club in town. Anyone who's anyone will be there. You up for it?"
"You bet." I looked down at my sweats and fuzzy slippers. "Just give me a few and I'll be ready."

"Terrific. I'll be home in a jiff."

All thoughts of the incongruities of the apartment, the overheard conversation between Bruce and Trevor, and the mystery waiting on my computer fled. I was ready for a really good time. As I was dressing, a voice in the back of my head kept whispering, *Enjoy it while you can.*

CHAPTER FIVE

Now there was plenty of work for me to do at the company, and I loved it, but I also longed to be sent on a trip. I had psyched myself into asking Sparrow about it when an interoffice memo popped up on my monitor. *Please see me immediately. —Sparrow.*

Excitement tingled throughout my whole body. Was this my first "Hit the Road" or "Skies" assignment? *Wait. Sky? Airplanes? I forgot about that part.* Now the tingling was mixed with stone cold fear at the prospect of flying.

I picked myself up, brushed off my black silk suit and Chinese red blouse. Steeling my nerves, I marched into her office.

There she stood in her Marilyn Monroe wanna-be posture. "Hello, Egypt," she said in her deep, cool voice. "You're booked for California next week. It's a modest assignment to get you started. Nothing too big or deeply serious."

California? That's across the country. Airplane. My throat went dry but I managed to squeak out a "Thanks."

"We need you to drop something off."

There was something steely cold in her eyes, as if they could kill by rolling in a certain way—like dice that just rolled on forever. As she looked at me, I was sure the temperature in the room dropped to freezing. I wondered if she was that way all the time, like a robot that dropped acid.
"That's about it," she said with a red-lipped smile that didn't quite reach her eyes. She handed me an envelope with all the information I needed—itinerary, flight, and so forth. She lowered her voice to a near whisper. "And, Egypt, we want to keep this low key—not attract a lot of attention."

Somehow that annoyed me. I already knew that when dealing with antiquities, it's always a good idea to keep it on the low-down. I had to do a good job with this "starter" assignment. I had my eye on other directions. This was a launching point for a bigger scope in my career. And, hell, how bad could it be? It was sunny California.

She turned as if to dismiss me. I cleared my throat. "I understand. In this business, one can't be too careful." I left quietly.

In the hallway, it struck me. *If they want to be so low-key, what are they doing in New York City? Hmmm. Maybe because this is where the money is?*

I couldn't wait to tell Gina.

***

At home, I rushed in, full of anticipation. "Gina?"
"In here," she called from the living room.

She was splayed out on the couch, feet up on the ottoman, watching *Top Model* on the giant plasma TV. Her purple silk lounging pajamas matched perfectly with her feathered slippers.

"Hi there," she said, clicking the remote to mute.

"Well, you didn't have to get all dressed up for me." I laughed.

"Huh. Very funny. Fashion isn't my *whole* life. I did spend a year in college, you know."

She glanced at the floor where her Gucci, suede boots with spike heels and silver toe-cap leaned against the couch. After seeing my expression, she gazed at me defiantly. "They come in very handy at times."

23

I certainly didn't understand that statement but decided to let it alone. "Okay. Whatever you say." I moaned. "Gina, I have great news!"

"What? Did Trevor ask you out?"

"Uh, no. I'm going to California next week and I'm taking you with me. Here's my itinerary, flight number, hotel reservation, and so forth. So book your seat on the flight and reserve a room in my hotel. We leave Tuesday."
Gina's eyes lit up like a kid with her first ice cream cone. "That's great! I'll get right on it." She started muttering under her breath about what clothes she needed. "Let's see, that gives me three days to prepare. Hmmm. Yes, I can do that."

She started to dash out of the room then stopped and looked back. "Wait, Egypt. You need new clothes. You simply can't go to California and look like a tourist." She scanned me up and down. "Now, let's have a look."

I didn't know whether to laugh or cry. "Hey, I'm not that bad." Her scowl let me know that arguing would do no good.

"Change, now. We're going shopping for one outfit to go in. We'll hit the Beverly Hills boutiques out there. My treat—anything you want but on one condition—I pick them out." She circled me muttering. "With your approval, naturally. But, really, admit it, you need my input." She plucked at my blouse. "You have fairly good taste, but you could use a bit more flair."

"Whatever you say, Gina. I kneel at the feet of the fashion master, the design queen."

"True." She put a finger to her chin. "Yes. I'm a clothing guru." She laughed. "Memorize that and burn it into your grey matter."

***

At the airport, I was fine until the last minute when we began that long trip through the passenger walkway. Tension mounted but I forced myself to keep going.

The flight attendant greeted us and pointed to first class. "Just over there."

I froze. Fortunately, Gina grabbed my hand, thanked the attendant, and then pulled me toward our seats. "Get a grip Egypt." She reached into her bag and shoved two pills into my hand. Take these."

I gave her a blank stare.
Gina hissed, "Now."

I popped them into my mouth and swallowed hard. I had to do my job, no matter what. I just kept telling myself, *Go girl. Do your thing.* I gripped the arm rests and tried, unsuccessfully, to control my heaving breath.

After a few minutes, my breathing slowed and my eyes grew heavy. "Hey, Gina, I'm shtartin' ta feel budder." *Oh, God, I sound drunk. But at least I'm not as scared as I was. Maybe I'd better take another pill—just in case this wears off too soon.*

I turned my head toward Gina and grinned like a sot. "Saay, pally. How 'bout one more?"

Gina flashed a warning glance. "Shhh. Close your eyes and relax."

I did, and soon I was sound asleep. The next thing I knew, Gina was gently shaking my shoulder.

"Wake up. We're here."

I slowly opened my eyes. My mouth tasted like cotton. While the others were standing to disembark, I rummaged in my bag for a Tic Tac. Pouring about four of them into my mouth, I was ready to get started on my assignment.

***

As we rushed out of the terminal, Gina pulled us to a taxi.

I gave the driver the address. We had to finish the assignment pronto.

He turned and looked at us, a question on his face. "You sure?"

I checked the address again. "Yes. That's the place."

He shrugged, set the meter, and we were on our way.

After about twenty minutes of driving through back streets we came to an old building. It was dirty with weathered, tan paint. A few vagrants loitered outside, bottles wrapped in paper. Two men sat near the stairs, talking to each other. One gave us a toothless grin when the taxi pulled up.

"Why would Eternal Treasures send you here?" asked Gina with a quaver in her voice. "I…I don't know. This looks dangerous. Maybe we should go to the hotel first. You could call your office and confirm the address." She shuddered.

"This *is* the address. I agree, it's unexpected, but my job might depend on it. So I'm going in—with or without you."

Gina reached into her bag and pulled out a bottle of hand sanitizer. "It's not that I'm myso…mysope… . You know the word you taught me about germs?"
"Mysophobic? Afraid of germs? Fine. We'll bathe in it afterwards if you want, but for Anubis' sake, we have to go."

She paid the taxi driver and asked him to wait.

26

The driver shook his head. "Not a chance. Gotta cell phone? Call another cab."

We watched him drive away, tires screeching on the pavement.

Gina stood outside the door, frozen like a mannequin. "Oh, mother-of-pearl I don't know. I'm going to get my clothes all smelly and dirty. We don't know what's really in there."

My patience was wearing. I just wanted to get in, do my job, and get the hades out of there. "Gina, you could stay outside with these gentlemen," I extended my arm toward the homeless men, "or you can come inside with me."

She bit her lip.

I noticed that our discomfort was a source of amusement to the vagrants but they made no move toward us and they said nothing. They just grinned and blinked.

"All right, all right. I'll go in. There's no chance I'm hanging out here, alone."

I turned the ancient handle opening the sagging, wooden door. Inside the lobby, the cracked black and white tiles were littered and dirty. I spotted a directory on the right-hand wall. To my surprise and relief, Eternal Treasures was listed— 202.

Not willing to risk the decrepit-looking elevator, we made our way up creaking stairs to the second floor, avoiding the none-too-clean looking handrail. "It's this way," I pointed to the left. "202." The company name was etched into the glass insert in the door. I turned to Gina. "The package I'm supposed to deliver is in this Target bag." I pulled it out of my large purse and held it up.
Gina's brow creased. "I wondered why you insisted on bringing that particular bag. What's in it?"

I shrugged "I don't know, when they X-rayed it at the airport, it just looked like a small, empty vase of some kind." In the corner of my mind, I knew something was contained within it.

Turning the handle, I cautiously stepped inside. Looking around I saw that although the furnishings and decor were probably pre-world war two, the room was clean and semi-well lit.

"May I help you?"

I jerked around. A woman, who could have been Bun Babe's twin came out of an inner office and sat behind the front desk.

"Uh. Yes." Was this a joke? No. "I'm Egypt Briggs. I'm here to deliver a package to Martin Cloud."
She picked up the old rotary phone handset with her delicate hand then pushed a button.

Gina found her way to an over-stuffed velvet chair and settled in, but not before she spread a handkerchief on it. "I'll just wait here," she said as she pulled a mirror out of her enormous bag and set to touching up her make up.

Bun Babe II cradled the phone. "You may go in." She gestured toward the door to her left.

I turned the cut-glass doorknob and stepped inside. *Wow!* Martin Cloud reclined behind a huge 18th century French Provincial Regency walnut desk. Spotless oak narrow-board flooring was topped with a magnificent caucus rug, its geometric designs bright and immaculate. On the bright, white walls, hung three bas reliefs—one Greek, depicting the abduction of Helen, one Egyptian scene of an afterlife judgment, and a third from ancient Rome, featuring Marcus Aurelius.

I was entranced, forgetting about Mr. Cloud, until I heard him clear his throat. I blinked and focused on him. Muscular, blond and handsome. *Are all the men at Eternal Treasures like Adonis?*

"Good Afternoon, Miss. . . . May I call you Egypt?"

He looked at me expectantly.

Aware that I was gawking, I coughed and handed him the package. "Sorry. Yes. Egypt is fine. Thank you for asking. I was just admiring your office."
"Miss Bawker, my receptionist, told me another young woman accompanied you."
"Yes. Gina is my friend. She wanted to come to California to shop and sightsee. I hope you don't mind that she's here."

"Not at all."

He examined the package then seemed to remember something. "Oh, yes. I have something Bruce wanted me to give you as a token of the company's appreciation on your first mission." He handed me a small box.

When I lifted the lid, I saw a gold necklace with an engraving of the peace sign. "Oh, this speaks to my hippie heart."

"Glad you like it. Now, let's take a look at the package you brought." He opened it carefully. "I know how this was delivered might seem unconventional, but I assure you there was good reason for it." He glanced up at me and smiled. "You didn't carry anything illicit."

He lifted out a perfect, colorful Italian vase.

"Thank you, Egypt. This is just what I was expecting. Perhaps we will see you again on your next trip."

"My pleasure." I turned and left the office. Gina, obviously bored, was staring at the ceiling. I called a taxi. We both waited behind the exit door of the building for what seemed like an eternity before it arrived.
When I heard the horn sound on the street, I grabbed her hand and yanked her out of the chair.

"Hey. Not so hard."

I just wanted out of that building and away from there. I nearly shoved Gina into the cab.

"Finally!" she said with relief as the driver pulled away. Gina gave him instructions to take us to Rodeo Drive, Beverly Hills. "Time for shopping!" She clapped her hands like a little girl at Christmas expecting a walking doll.

***

Gina dragged me from store to store like a lifeless rag doll. It's not that I didn't love shopping in the famous Beverly Hills, I was tired. The three-hour time difference was starting to kick in. We had lunch at the very famous Spago's and were treated like royalty. I wondered how the maître d' knew her by name even though we didn't have a reservation. I soon discovered that her family had connections there. I was impressed but mostly glad to be off my feet.

After lunch, it was more shopping. From street to street and window to window we chugged like locomotives on a mercy mission. She managed to wrestle me into the lingerie department. She picked up a piece of material and held it in front of me. It was miniscule. I thought it must have been ripped from something.

"What the hell is that?" I questioned her.

"It's one of a girl's best buddies. They're thong panties, E.G., get with the program!"

I drew the line at thong panties, though. Ewww. We bought everything from shoes to lingerie, practical, but pretty lingerie.

After a while, I had the strange feeling that we were being watched. My senses on high alert, I asked Gina, "Have you noticed anything like, maybe someone behind us while we were shopping?"

"Uh-huh. Why? Is it something I should be concerned about?"

"Dear, sweet Gina. Of course it is. You wait here for a minute and pretend you're looking in the window while I do something."

"Okay."

She struck a pose as if she was considering something in the display. I casually walked down the street and when I knew the time was right, I whirled around and caught the stalker standing by a shop window. He looked like a short Joe Palooka with a cigar. "Okay Mr. Jokester. What the hell are you doing following us?"

"Hey, lady," he said shrugging his shoulders. "What's your problem? I'm just walking here. I ain't followin' nobody."

"Sure. For over an hour, you're everywhere we are. I want some answers."
"Like I said, I ain't followin' nobody. Maybe you're following me." He stuck out his chin and chewed on his cigar while laughing.

Out of the blue, I looked both ways, and then I rammed my fist into his solar plexus. He wasn't expecting that, and it

31

knocked the wind out of him. He slid down the window like sludgy rainwater.

I brushed my hands off and walked back to Gina. "Hey, I know you saw me do that. I think he was following us because he smelled money. As soon as we were out of sight of the shops, I bet he was going to mug us."
Gina's eyes were as wide as saucers but all she said was, "Okay. Are we going to finish shopping, or what?"

I had to laugh. "Sure. Let's go."
"Well, now *I'm* tired," said Gina. I'm ready to go back to the hotel. She punched in a number on her cell. I'm having a car from the hotel pick us up."

***

"Wonderful. I'm ready, too. How long will it take?"

"Just a few minutes. We can wait on the bench over there."

We walked to a bench in front of a shop and sat. "I'm really glad I had the stores send our purchases to the hotel. We couldn't possibly carry all that stuff."
My stomach growled. "If I don't get a hot fudge sundae soon, I might die. Do you think the hotel kitchen can make one for me?"

"If they don't, there'll be hell to pay. I don't want to be around you if you're denied a good dose of hot fudge. It's your feel good medicine." She laughed. "No pizza?" she questioned. "Strange."

We spent our waiting time talking about our purchases and what a great day we had.

"There's the car." Gina stood and pulled me to my feet. A limo pulled to the curb and the driver got out, rounded the car and opened the door for us.

"Thank you, um..." I read his name tag, "George."

***

As soon as we settled into our suite, I kicked off my shoes and called room service. One hot fudge sundae would be mine in ten minutes. Ahhh.

Gina joined me in the living room. Her brow creased and she pulled on her lower lip. "Cripes, Egypt. Why do you think that man was following us today?"

"Like I told you. He was looking to mug us. But we'll probably never really know." I shuddered. "He looked like he could have been one of Freddie Krueger's crew."

"Humph. That's all we need." She reached for the phone. "I'm calling room service for a sub. Interested?"
"I'd rather have a small pizza to chase down my hot fudge sundae." I smiled and tousled her hair.

"Ah, now this is the real Egypt. Pizza."

CHAPTER SIX

After all the excitement of the trip, and after working until the end of the week, I spent Saturday relaxing in my apartment. Gina was gone all day and I had a lot of time to think. My family crept into my head and guilt seeped in.

The only people in my family I truly trusted were Uncle Max and Grandpa. I wondered if Mom told them that I'd left town and gotten a job in New York. Yeah, she must have. My family is pretty traditional. A woman stays at home until married. For me, that would have been a death sentence, especially with the slim choice of men there. I had to leave.

Uncle Max always told me to "Go for it." He retired from police work after a job injury—a bullet in the knee. He never flinched from anything thrown his way. When I was a kid, it was Uncle Max who took me to karate classes. Mom thought martial arts weren't something a lady should be doing. He told me that a woman could never be too careful—or too nimble.

Grandpa Yagelska is stubborn, opinionated, and built like a hot brick oven. In spite of his age, he's really strong. His hair is only sprinkled with silver and he looks much younger than he is. Only a few crease-lines around his mouth and brow give him away. He's strict and stern. He has a look that says, "You're in trouble, now." It always stopped me in my tracks.

That phone book incident scared the salesman half to death—enough to guarantee three years of free ads. His look alone would have done it.

Dad has a good heart and the patience of a saint. He had to have this trait to put up with Mom all these years. No matter what she does, he just accepts it with a smile. Such love.

CHAPTER SEVEN

Still no more assignments, so I decided to study the cryptic file again. *If I just stare at it long enough I know something will start to make sense.*

After an hour, nothing. It still looked like something from Mars. *Maybe I'm being paranoid. Maybe I should tell Bruce I've seen it.* Something stopped me, though. I sighed while pushing back from my desk and proceeded strolling to the lounge for a cup of coffee. Coming back while approaching my door, I noticed an envelope on the floor.

"What?" Picking it up, I saw there was no name on it and the envelope wasn't sealed. I felt it with my fingers. Lumpy. *Hmmm.*

I opened it. Inside was a note, a flash drive, and a pair of ear buds. The note read:

Listen, but not here. Go to an Internet café or the Library.

You have a friend.

No signature.

This is exciting. Maybe it has something to do with the cryptic file and the conversation I overheard between Bruce and Trevor. And, who sent this?

I couldn't wait to get out of there. No one would miss me for at least a couple of hours, so I slipped out the exit leading to the stairs and headed for The Daily Grind coffee place around the corner. It had a few seldom used computers for the public.

After ordering a large mocha latté and getting the pass code for one of the computers, I settled in, slipped the flash drive into the USB slot and inserted the ear buds into the sound port.

At first there was the crackle of papers, or some indefinable noise, and then I heard Bruce's voice.

It's time we ramped up the plan. I'm hoping everything falls in our direction. Since our enemy and rivals follow our every fake move, like we planned, this should make them think we know they're close and that we're running scared. Hah. This gives us the upper hand. Nothing like clever deception.

That's definitely Bruce's voice.

There was a pause and some shuffling noise then he was speaking again.

This isn't without risk. Those bastards fixed it so the Russian mob believes we stole the goods. We're dealing with obstacle after obstacle they fling our way. They believe if we're apprehensive and threatened we might fold. Then, we turn the tables.
I think they know us better than that. We've battled before, Bruce, but the Russians? How do you know it's the Russians?

So, that's Trevor with him.

I've had my suspicions for a while. They were confirmed yesterday, when I got a threatening call on my private number. Deep Russian accent. They believe we are moving in on their territory and are planning to take over their operation. Cryptonomics is behind that one for certain.

Since we hired Egypt and will be recruiting her friend, Gina, it gives us an advantage. On assignment, they look like two beautiful women vacationing, shopping, and sightseeing instead of delivering the goods. They have to be kept in the dark about what their real mission is.

I agree. What did you tell the Russian?

I told them the truth. We had nothing to do with it and Crypto was out to destroy us. They didn't believe me. So, thanks to Crypto, our plans have to take a detour.

I heard the sound of that creaky door. I was digesting the part about recruiting Gina at this point.
They are welcoming Joey now. I wonder what his part is in the scheme of things.

Joey! Come in. Bruce and I are going over the plan. Looks like Crypto might take our bait. We made it seem like we'd put up roadblocks to them getting anymore intel from us and that we planted information to make them doubt what they thought they knew. They have no idea how much money we've raised. Feeding them bits will make them think they can defeat us. Hopefully they'll believe they are wrong about the location. They have come too close for comfort, and safety.

There were a few seconds of silence before Trevor continued:

It's not without risk. If they discover our deception everything could blow up in our faces. They know for sure that we have the critical scriptures.

Joey:

Our people are on top of it. That's what I came to tell you.

Hmm, big boss is responding.

Good. I have to smile when I think of those asses shriveling from all their work in the Egyptian sun. They'll be living and working in the hottest hell possible, inhaling dust that will deliver nothing. They've taken every piece of false info we've fed them. If they discover the truth, it won't be pretty. That's why this move is important, even though it means we'll be excavating close to the enemy. We'll just have to keep our eyes and ears open and proceed with extreme caution.

Trevor:

If Crypto wins, the whole earth is in danger. The devil is in them, that is for sure. We can't let them find the instrument first and turn it into a weapon!

You are so right, my friend. We can't take a chance that they—or anyone else—will get to the instrument in her tomb. I call it the great "Bubble Ripper." But maybe "blaster" is more like it.

I could hear Joey's tension clearly.

I can see all those skidder-sleds with their death-beams, weapons of obedience, and more. I'm sure every world leader would fall in line with them to save their own skins, but it might not matter. If Crypto gets a hold of the secrets in the tomb, civilization as we know it will end. The earth will be scorched but it will be theirs.

Trevor leaping in again.

That's why we must succeed. The huge time leap has changed the land enough forever and the device will be lost. As long as they assume they know where the tomb is, we'll be home free.

The ancients buried the device for a reason. To keep it out of the hands of people like Crypto. They figured the "Ripper" was safe. After all, everyone believes she's in her original tomb somewhere in Alexandria. The question I've had since we discovered this, who invented the damned thing in the first place? And why our ancestors thought it necessary to dabble in Earth's affairs."

The new and improved "Ripper" is meant to open a mammoth rip in the timeline allowing their hoards to enter, but since there's no way to really test it, they could be destroying the earth, too. We can only rely on our research... I, for one, am confident that our motivation to preserve life and keep the world in tact will win over their greed and need for ultimate power. Maybe they think they're all incarnations of the Caesars.

Let's make sure they end up as Caesar salad.

Wow, they have a sense of humor.

After a long silence, Joey bid them good-bye and said he'd get his ass in gear.

Static and the end of the file.

I just sat there, staring at the monitor. Chills ran through my body. *Oh my God!* I had no idea what to think. *Tomb? Hmmm.* This whole thing was confusing. I didn't understand what I had just heard. The only message that was loud and clear was that there was a weapon that could destroy the earth and we have to get to it first or *KABOOM!* Maybe I was in deeper than I should be. But then, if I keep this knowledge to myself, maybe I could help. *I'm just going to play dumb and see where this takes me. I'm not even sure I'll share this with Gina. That is, until she's on board.*

CHAPTER EIGHT

"Got a minute?" Trevor poked his head into my office.

"Of course. Come in."

He strode into the room and sat in the wing-back chair. I came out from behind my desk and sat on the sofa. "Well? I'm all ears."

He leaned back and crossed one leg over the other. "It looks like your first delivery job went pretty well—except for the thug who was following you."

"How in the world do you know about that?" My mind raced with strange thoughts. Was he following me? Didn't he trust me to do the job right?

"I guess I owe you an explanation. It's nothing sinister. Because it was your first trip, I thought it best to add a safety net for you. It's a pretty rough neighborhood, so I hired someone to keep a discrete eye on you. But when he saw what you did to the would-be mugger, he figured you could take care of yourself. He assured me that his services would not be needed."

"Uh, I don't know what to say about that. I'm not sure if I should be annoyed or grateful."

Trevor joined me on the sofa. "I apologize. It won't happen again. But, I am curious about one thing."

The hairs on my arms stood up as he sat down. *How embarrassing! A dashing man, and my hair is standing at attention*, I scolded myself.
Then alarms of caution flared in my brain. "And, what would that be?"

He returned to the chair. "The woman we saw you with, she's your roommate? Gina, isn't it?"

"She's my best friend. When she heard I was going to the L.A. area, she asked if she could come along to shop. She's kind of a shopping goddess. I hope you don't mind that she was there."

Leaning forward, Trevor looked into my eyes. A shiver of delight ran through my body. Those hairs hadn't calmed a bit.

"Not at all. In fact, Bruce and I talked about it at length after Martin called and suggested that you having a partner would be a good idea. It might make things look less suspicious if the two of you were together—shopping and sightseeing. It's a great deception. You see, many of the things we will have you delivering are for repatriation. It's good money and satisfying work. We don't want certain others to know how we make some of our bankroll. And, there's always the danger of the objects being stolen to sell on the black market."

Holy Horus-tearing eye. I was flabbergasted. This could work out really well. Gina and I together, having fun. "I agree with everything you said. She sometimes comes off as a bit of an air head, but I assure you that she's really earthy, honest, and smart. She just has an ongoing love affair with Chanel, Gucci, and a few other designers. Fashion is her hobby."

"So, do you think she would consider working for us?" asked Trevor.

"I don't know. I'll ask her tonight." *Hehehe, would she? No brainer.*

"Great." He stood starting for the door. "Oh, I almost forgot." He turned back to look at me. "There's a meeting coming up soon. We'll need your input, if possible. Sparrow will send

41

you the particulars. In the meantime, we might have another trip for you."

Wonderful. I love this. I walked over to him. "Oh?"

"Yes. This time you will be carrying an ancient treasure we intend to give back to its country. This is a touchy assignment, but I'm confident you can handle it."

I was unnerved. On one hand, I appreciated his confidence. On the other, it meant that I really had to live up to his expectations. After he left and the door was closed, my heart was thumping. I steadied my balance by clinging to the doorknob, inhaling slow, deep breaths until I felt I could safely return to my desk.

I wonder if this has anything to do with the conversation I listened to on that flash drive. What in the world was going on?

***

"Gina? Are you home?" Opening the door I scanned the apartment. The sofa in the living room was piled with colorful packages, bags, and boxes. *I guess she is home.*

"I'm here," she came into the room from the kitchen, holding a cup of tea. "Hey there. How was work today?"

I swept my hand through the air toward the buried sofa. "I see you've had a fun-filled day."

Her eyes got as large as saucers. "I'll just put these things into my bedroom."

I couldn't help but laugh. "No. It's okay." I laughed even harder when I saw relief on her face.

I wanted to find the right time to talk to her about what Trevor had said—and some other things, but I was starving. "How about some dinner? I'm chef tonight."

"I'd love that. I'm kind of pooped after shopping and was going to raid the refrigerator or call for delivery. I'd much rather have a home-cooked meal. You're the best."

After changing into a pair of jeans and a Tee, I tackled dinner, piling the counter with ingredients to make small burritos and tacos.

"Can I help?" Gina gave me the look that meant, please say no." She's a disaster. Oh, she can cook, but the kitchen looks like a tornado went through it. Every fork, bowl, and pan would be piled in the sink along with spills, crumbs, and packaging strewn everywhere. No thanks. "I've got this. You just relax and enjoy." I gave her a bright smile.
She settled onto one of the tall stools at the counter to watch me work.

"Gina, Trevor told me today that the office knew you went to California with me."

"And? It was on my dime, and I didn't interfere with your job. Is there a problem?"

"Oh, no. Nothing like that." This wasn't going to be easy. Gina with a *real* job? She had all the money she needed or wanted. Her part time flower shop job was only a few hours a week. I had to word this just right so she would think it was an adventure. Oh, hell, just say it straight. "Gina, they want you to work with me. You know, go on all the trips with me."

Gina's huge eyelashes flapped at me. She looked puzzled, but in a good way. "They want *me?*"

"Uh-huh. They think two women would look less obvious when we go on our trips," I made finger quotes in the air.

43

"Sightsee and shop." Focusing on seasoning the meat I began explaining. "They need an answer soon. I have another trip coming up."

She slipped off the stool and paced the kitchen. "Wow. This sounds daring. I mean, think about it. They want me, Gina Scarpetta." She tapped her chin. "And, it won't interfere with my shopping." A big grin was cut short by an open mouthed, silent "Oh, no."

"What?"

"What would my parents and Uncle say? My mother expects me home every Sunday for lasagna, and Uncle Quarto watches me like a hungry lion."

"Forget about Uncle Quarto. You're twenty-three now—and have all the money you want. It's time you made your own decisions."

Gina planted her fists on her hips and squared her shoulders. "You're right. It won't be *every* Sunday, right?"

"Right. You can always make excuses for the days you have to be gone on a Sunday. . . . And think of the shopping, and most likely the men!"

"I'll do it. Can I start on Monday? That way I can have my hair done and get a mani-pedi first. Oh, and I need to tell them at the flower shop that I won't be back. I want a brand new outfit for my first day too."

She went shopaholic on me to prepare for her new vocation - spy.

Relief spread through me like a dog after a bath. "I'll let Trevor know." Yep, it did turn out to be a no-brainer.

Gina peered into my eyes. "You really like him, don't you?"

44

I'm sure I turned shades of red. "Ya think? Still, I'm sure I don't have a chance in hell."

"What? You think you're not good enough for him? What's the matter with you? You're one hot woman and don't ever forget it. Go for it. He'd be lucky to have you."

I thought about the tripe passing for men I knew back home. "It's not that, well maybe it was a little until I thought about the guys I've known. Trevor towers over them body, mind, and soul." I shuddered. "When I think of the creeps I've dated…remember Gregory?"

"Yeah." Gina screwed up her face. "Makes me nauseous just thinking about that jerk." She brushed her fingers through her hair. "You deserve much better."

CHAPTER NINE

Gina lounged on the sofa in my office. Her long legs draped over the arm. "I'm bored."

"You don't like working here?" I asked looking up from my computer.

"Oh, the coffee is good. Not the cheap pre-ground stuff. *Definitely* Arabica. The pastries are de-lish. But I'm itchy to buy something exotic. I want to go on another adventure and feel like an international spy."

She sat up and rested her elbows on her knees, chin in hand.

"Gina, when we go, and where, is up to them. I won't know until almost the last minute. It's all classified—on the sly."

"Ooh, mysterious and clever." She tapped her chin. "Whatever our reason for going, I know shopping and men will be the best part. I'm good at that."
"Don't I know it," I rolled my eyes.

***

My inter-office memo pinged. It was Trevor.

"Egypt, would you come to my office, please?"

I stood, smoothed my skirt then checked my hair and make-up in the mirror I had stashed in my desk. My heart raced. *This could be it!*

When I entered his office, he stood in front of his desk in the pinstriped suit that I loved. His aftershave wafted toward me. *Mmmm. I bet this attracts women like lionesses in heat.*

"Egypt, come in."

He seemed nervous, fiddling with the pen in his hand. He avoided eye contact.

"Uh, sit down." He gestured toward a chair in front of the sofa. "I feel a bit awkward and I know this is a bit risky—because of our professional relationship—but I...I'm sure you know how much I like you, personally, I mean."

I just nodded. *What is he getting at?*
He pulled the matching chair around to face me. "With the company policy, I shouldn't even approach this, but I really have to or I will go crazy."

Yes. Get on with it. Ask me out, already.

"Trevor. Whatever you want to say is all right with me. I can keep a confidence." That seemed to help him relax a bit.

"Will you go out with me? This Friday?"

Even though I had been pretty sure of what he was going to say, when the words came out, I thought I might faint. He'd been flirtatious in a cautious way. I wasn't sure if he was just playing around or he was really attracted to me. Now I knew and I was almost speechless. *Get it together, girl.*

"Egypt? Did you hear me?"
"Uh, oh, well... of course. I'd love to. I was just a little surprised, that's all."

He let out a long breath. "That's great. I'll pick you up at seven. I have somewhere special in mind. There's no need to tell anyone else about this, yet. Okay?"

"I have to tell Gina."

"I meant anyone in the office. I know she works here, now, but you know what I mean, especially Bruce."

"Of course. I understand. Office gossip and all that."

He grinned and nodded. "Thanks."

After leaving his office, I leaned against the wall for a few seconds to gather my thoughts. I spotted Gina in the hallway and ran to her. Grabbing her arm, I whispered, "We need to talk."

"Huh?"

I led her into my office and shut the door. Pulling her onto the sofa to sit next to me, I spilled the whole story. "Gina, you'll never guess what happened."

"We're going on a mission?" She grinned.

"No. Trevor asked me out!"

"What?"

"We're going out this Friday."

"No kidding. I would never have guessed." She feigned nonchalance.

"You knew?"

"Well, I didn't *know,* but I'm Italian and have a second sense about these things. I saw the way he stared at you when you weren't looking."

"And, you didn't warn me?"

"Why should I? I knew you'd say yes. Congrats. He's a good one. And what do you mean *warn*?"

"Since when did you develop psychic powers," I teased.

"Remember Gregory? That nimrod. I knew he wasn't right for you—and you almost married him. And, remember when I predicted that Eva would win a cool thousand in the lottery? I could smell money." She lifted her chin in defiance of any denial.

"Okay, so you're psychic. Now, he didn't say where we're going, but I'm sure it will be somewhere special. What should I wear?"

My office door opened and Bruce stepped in. "Hi." He nodded to me then to Gina. "Girl talk? Oh, sorry. It didn't sound so sexist in my head." He blushed and grinned.

"Hi Bruce. What can I do for you?" I stood and offered him a chair at my desk.

"Thanks, but this will only take a minute. We have an assignment for you next week." Turning to Gina, he asked, "Is your passport in order? We need both of you to go to Rome for a delivery."

Gina nearly shot off the sofa. "Rome? In Italy? Oooh. Yes! My passport and credit card are always ready. No problem there."

"Great. I'll send over the details. Sparrow and Myrtle will coordinate your transportation and reservations. *Ciao!"* He turned and left.

After the door closed, I ran to Gina and hugged her. "Rome!" *Thank God I did get a passport.*

***

I paced my bedroom. It hit me that I would be going out with Trevor, alone, with no one else around. Biting my lip, fear set in. *Stop it, Egypt. This is no time to flinch. Get yourself together.* I poked my head out my bedroom door. "Gina? I need your help."

"I'm coming," she called from the living room. In a few seconds she was in my room.

"So, you need my advice about dating wear, I assume."

"Of course. I'm scared to death."

"I know I've been attracted to several men since we came here, but there's something different about Trevor. It's like he has substance. He's not only great looking, he has something more."
She put a finger to pursed lips. "Well, first, let me take a look at your wardrobe." She started for my closet when her cell rang. "Sorry, I have to get this. It's Mike."

Mike was someone she recently met at a club. In my opinion, she was too attached to him, too soon. I'd only met him twice and didn't feel good about him—too secretive and a bit pushy. I just had to trust that Gina would catch on to his game and kick him to the curb.

After she hung up, she turned back to me. Her face was flushed. "Okay, where were we?"

"My wardrobe."

"Oh, yes." She started moving my dresses along the closet rod, examining each one. "So, what did Trevor say when he asked you out?"

"In a nutshell, he said that in spite of the company policy, he had to ask me. He said he had somewhere special in mind."

"Hmmm. Special? Could be an exclusive restaurant, or a Broadway show. Well, either way, let's go for something *uber*

50

sexy. Here," she pulled out the Vera Wang dress she bought me in Beverly Hills. "Navy is just the color to bring out your eyes."

"I was hoping for a chance to wear this." I touched the soft fabric."

"Shoes. These are perfect." She placed the silver Blahniks on the bed next to the dress. Then she strode over to my jewelry chest. "And," she lifted out the silver Deco watch and my diamond earrings. "If this doesn't make his eyes pop out of his head, nothing will."

I was dazzled at her expertise. "This is beautiful, Gina. But do you think it a bit too sexy for a first date?"

She glared at me. "Hey, bestie. Do you trust my instincts, or not? There is never too sexy when I'm in charge."

I had to admit, she was right. After all, fashion is more than a hobby for Gina—it's her life's work. She has so many clothes, she stores most of them in a rented locker. She keeps a complicated list of the contents so she can plan what she'll wear to any event.

"Thanks," I said, giving her a hug. "I'm going to take a shower, then get dressed."

"Anytime." Grinning in obvious satisfaction, she marched out of the room.

***

At seven sharp, the doorbell rang. Gina answered and ushered him into the living room. I had been ordered by my fashion goddess and dating guru to let him wait at least five minutes. I stood at the door of my bedroom staring at my watch. After four minutes, the second hand seemed to drag on forever. "Five!" I whispered and opened the door.

Casually striding into the living room, I said, "Sorry to keep you waiting. Ready?"

He just stood there, eyes wide. Dressed in a camel-colored cashmere sweater with a navy jacket and slacks, I nearly melted at how amazing he was.

Nervously, he thrust a small bouquet of flowers at me. "For you," he said. "You look stunning."

I took the flowers. "Oh, thank you. They're lovely."

Gina came into the room at the exact right time. "Here, I'll put these in water. You two have a good time," she said, sounding decidedly older sister-ish.

Outside, a cab was waiting. Climbing in with his old-fashioned gentlemanly help, he closed the door and rounded the back of the car to get in on the other side. "I hope you like where I'm taking you."

He scanned me from head to toe and looked a bit worried.

"I'm sure it will be lovely." *I hope it's not French. I'm not fond of all that sauce and dishes I can't pronounce. Maybe Chinese? It's easier to pick out the pieces I don't like. Stop being so picky, Egypt. Shut up and enjoy yourself.*
The cab rolled to a stop. Trevor paid the driver then hurried around to open my door. Getting out was treacherous in my sparkly Blahniks. Looking up I saw that we were in front of a Pizza place. I gulped and almost bolted. I looked around hoping there was a classy place nearby. Nope. This was it. I wanted to die. I was *extremely* overdressed for pizza.

"Surprised?" he said forcing a smile. "Myrtle told me pizza is one of your favorite foods. She said you order enough to run a service out of the office."

His laugh was nervous and I knew he must be regretting his decision to bring me here—and rightfully so.

"I hope I did the right thing." He looked at me expectantly.

I took a deep breath and smiled. "No. It's fine. She's right. I love pizza." *Easy girl, he tried to get it right. I'll have to kill Myrtle, though.* "How sweet of you." *Sure. It'll be like eating Brussels sprouts, i.e. Green Marbles, when everyone else is having turkey. Speaking of turkeys, I sure "dressed" up like one for this very casual occasion.*

He offered me his arm and we walked into the Kesté Pizza & Vino. It wasn't as rustic as I was expecting. Pretty nice actually. The hardwood floors and clean atmosphere wasn't like any pizza joint I'd ever been in. Heavenly is the only word for the intoxicating aroma of spices emanating from the kitchen.

"Trevor!" said a man in a brown T-shirt as he came out of the kitchen. "How are you, my friend?"

"Roberto. Good to see you. This is Egypt, a special friend."

Ah, so he also likes Italian. Sounds like a frequent customer.

The man smiled and took my hand. "Welcome." He looked around. "Here. Here is a good table for you."

"Thanks," said Trevor.

Roberto nodded and ducked back into the kitchen to man a gleaming copper pizza oven.

"Well?" asked Trevor looking hopeful."

"Nice. Really good choice."

He relaxed.

I still felt a bit self-conscious. Even though this was a really nice place, the other people in there were dressed in casual clothes. I saw a woman a couple of tables over glance at me then say, "How cute," to her companion. A few others looked at me with what I read as friendly curiosity. I soon forgot my state of overdress and enjoyed the most incredible pizza I had ever eaten.

"Wow," I stated after munching down the last crumb of a perfect crust. "That was unbelievably good."

We finished off our wine then Trevor said goodbye to Roberto and we left. The evening was cool and beautiful.

"Mind if we walk a bit?" asked Trevor.

"Not at all," I lied, thinking about my beautiful but torturous shoes. He must have read my mind.

"Well, maybe a walk could wait until a time when you aren't balancing on those?" He smiled.

I laughed. "Thanks. I agree."

He hailed a cab and gave the driver directions to an address I didn't recognize. A little while later, we were standing in front of a sweet shoppe sporting the lovely and appropriate name, Decadent Delights.

Trevor looked over at me and raised his eyebrows. "Live dangerously? You won't regret it."

"I never reject an opportunity for a hot fudge sundae!" This place had my name written all over it and was calling me like a lost baby screaming for its momma.

While Trevor dove into a banana split, I was in ecstasy with my Brownie Sundae. I nearly fainted, it was so good. We talked like old friends who had known each other a lifetime. It was so easy and comfortable, yet an exciting tension filled me. We talked about everything except work.

What a fascinating man. Who knew he was so real—aside from being hot. I learned that he was a voracious reader, never had a pet but liked animals—except snakes.

"I'm a cat person. Dogs are fine, but cats are mysterious and fascinating. I lost my Samson last year. He was one of the bright lights in my life."

I watched to see if he would tease me about felines. He didn't. Instead he reached over and touched my hand.

"I'm sorry. It's hard to lose someone you care about."

He understands! This guy gets better by the minute. I told him that my first love was Egypt—the country, not me—and that I hoped to write a book about it one day, or even participate in an archaeological dig there.

"Bravo. You set your sights high. I'm not much of a writer myself. I'm in awe of anyone with that kind of talent."

"Trevor, you have many talents of your own."

***

Trevor walked me to my door. He stood close and I backed up against the wall. I wanted to throw my arms around him and drag him inside, but knew a little restraint would be the best thing to practice right now. Still it was hard to ignore the sparks exploding inside me.
When he leaned in, I thought I would combust. But he planted a sweet kiss on my cheek.

"Thanks, Egypt. I had a wonderful evening."

"I did, too. Goodnight."

He touched my cheek. "Goodnight."
I watched him walk away, fantasizing about us tumbling in my purple-satin sheets. *Stop it.* I unlocked the door and went inside.

Gina's Mike was just leaving. He gave me a wink as he passed. *I don't like that guy.*

Gina hurried to me as soon as Mike shut the door behind him. "How was your date?"

She eyed my dress. "What's that stain?" She sniffed the air around me. You smell like pizza! Tell me it isn't true."

"It actually wasn't that bad. The pizza place was really good, even elegant in a way. Now, I'm really tired.
Can we talk about this in the morning?"

"Sure, honey. Get some rest."

***

In the morning, Gina had coffee, croissants with French butter and gourmet strawberry jam waiting for me.

"Ooh. Thanks. What's the occasion?"

"Nothing. I just thought you deserved it, that's all."

"Gina, I know you. What happened? Is it Mike?"

She sipped her coffee. "Maybe."

"Spill it. You know I did some snooping around about him, myself."

"Well, the jerk asked me for a favor. You know he's always asking me for favors. This time it was money and I told him I had to think about it. He got pretty nasty and tried to intimidate me."

"So?"

"So I kicked him to the curb. I won't be seeing him anymore...creep!"

I could see that she was disappointed. Men often took advantage of her because of her money. Some men couldn't see beyond her wallet and physical beauty. Gina was an amazing woman—kind, generous, funny, loyal, and so many things. I wanted to tie Mike, the loser, up by his thumbs and set him on fire.

CHAPTER TEN

I had a few days before leaving for Rome so I took a little time to revisit the mysterious file.

"Hey Gina, want to look at this weird thing I told you I found on my computer when I first came to work here."

"Sure. I've been thinking about that lately."

She pulled up a chair next to me and peered at the image on my monitor. "Any clue about what those symbols might mean?"

I shrugged. "I don't really know but it must be a code of some kind."

"Do you suppose it could be something to do with the computer itself?" Gina leaned closer to the image.

"I doubt it. Nothing else seems to be affected. But, maybe we could poke around at some of the other computers and see if we can uncover anything unconventional."

Gina leaned back in her chair. "Sounds like a good plan, but what about all the security cameras?"

"I can come in early tomorrow." I glanced at the door. "There's something about the supply room that calls to me. I'm not sure what, and it doesn't make logical sense, but my gut tells me to go there and search for anything out of the ordinary."

"Great," said Gina. You could pretend you are looking for supplies. Hmmm. Let me think." She pouted her lips and rested her chin on her hand. "I have it. Walk in carrying a gift box with a bow on it. Pretend you're looking for somewhere to hide it. You could put a note inside thanking Trevor for last night. The wonderful evening you had."

"That's brilliant. What a team we make." I turned off the monitor. "Gina, I just realized that whenever I mentioned work to Trevor on our night out, he sidestepped the issue. Well, we'll just keep digging and the beans shall come forth." We both had a good laugh. I thought that I already had some of the "beans" and was keeping my mouth shut. Outside of me, Gina was the only other person who knew about the recording.

"Plus those conversations you overheard and the recording. Did you ever find out who slipped that under your door?"

"No. I have my suspicions, though. I can't talk about it yet. I want to be sure, first."

"So, we get to work really early tomorrow?"
"You bet."

***

The next morning we awoke at 4am. I don't know how she does it. Even with a serious lack of sleep and at the crack of dawn, Gina looked like a queen. Not a hair out of place. I looked like the dawn of death.
I did my best, yawning and trying to keep my eyes open. Grabbing the box we wrapped the night before and my key card, we headed for the office.

The sun was just coming up when we opened the front door of Eternal Treasures. The night guard looked at us with curiosity.

"Good morning, ladies," he said as we signed in. "Getting an early start, I see."

"Yes, Jeff. Big project coming up and I want to hide this gift before anyone else comes in."

He winked. "I understand."

We trekked down the long hallway to the supply room and cracked open the door. One wall was full of computers. They looked the same as the one in my office. I put down the box and found an extension power strip to plug the computers in. I wanted to find out if there was anything different about them that would give us a clue to the strange writing.

"Plug in a few of those, will you Gina?" I whispered.

After a moment, six computers came to life. It turned out that they were all password protected and locked. I couldn't get in. "Damn!" As I looked at the computers, I did notice that they looked like more powerful models than the one I used. But, without getting in, I couldn't really say how I knew this.

"Hey," whispered Gina. "I think there's a door back here." I unplugged the computers and stashed the power strip into the box it came from then joined Gina. "That's odd. It's wedged into a corner. I've never seen anything like it."

"And, look. There's a padlock."

"Hmmm. That is strange. I mean, the building next door couldn't be more than a foot or so from ours." I glanced at my watch. "We'd better go. I pushed the gift box behind a computer then cracked the door. "Clear. Let's go."

Gina and I stepped into the hallway as if everything was perfectly normal. "We have to find a way to investigate that door," I said.

"We'll figure it out. No worries."
An hour later, I retrieved the package and headed for Trevor's office. Standing in front of his closed door, I started

to doubt that this was a good idea. *Will he read too much into this? What if he doesn't like what I bought him? Maybe it's too soon. Oh! Egypt, stop whining and go in. How could he not like the crystal sail boat I found at Greene's Antique shop?*

I mustered my courage and knocked.

"Come."

I opened the door. "Hi Trevor. I—"

"Egypt. Come in." He eyed the gift box. "What's that?"

"It's a little present for you." I handed it to him.
He carried it to his desk. "Shall I open it now?"

"Oh, please do."

He carefully untied the ribbon and lifted the lid. Before he opened the tissue inside, he read the note. His smile was all I needed to feel reassured that I had done the right thing.

"I had a wonderful evening, too. Next time we'll make it somewhere besides a pizza place," he teased me with a twinkle lighting up his eyes.

"Oh, the pizza was the best. It's just not what I had expected, that's all."

He gently took out the crystal sail boat. "Egypt! This is amazing. How did you know I like sail boats?"

I glanced at the photo on his desk of him on a three-masted schooner. His hair blowing in the wind and looking like he'd just found heaven. "It wasn't difficult."

"Thank you." He placed it on his desk and studied it. "It's perfect." He looked up. Well, I guess you're off to Italy tomorrow. All packed?"

"Almost. My flight leaves at seven in the morning so I'll be up at dawn."

"I, we'll miss you around here. Have a wonderful time. Rome is beautiful."

"Thanks, I will." I left his office walking with a lilt. He wasn't mine, yet, but I had hopes for the future. *The planets will align for us and we'll be right under them to bask in their beauty.*

Back in my office, I opened the cryptic file, again. I tried a few things to decode it but failed. *Damn. I'm not good enough at this. I'll have to call my cousin Reggie again. I think he's stalling. Cripes, maybe he forgot? If anyone can tell me what's going on he should be able to, I think.*
My phone buzzed and my attention was changed.

"Yes?" It was Bruce.

"Egypt would you and Gina join us in a meeting in my office?"

"Of course. Now?"

"Yes. Thanks."

I knew there was an important meeting this morning but didn't remember that they wanted us there.

We hurried to Bruce's office. The others were already there. I took a seat on the sofa. Gina sat next to me.

Bruce's serious voice echoed over the buzz of the room. "I'm glad to see all of you here for the announcement I am about to make."

I looked around. Bonnie from filing and two programmers were there—Lisa and Kelly. Kelly was so young I was sure he hadn't even begun to shave. I spotted our appraiser, Larry, and Dina and Joey from accounting. Joey was another odd one. He rarely spoke to anyone and wouldn't make eye contact when he did. One exception seemed to be Gina. Bun Babe was conspicuously missing. *I guess she was elected to answer the phones. There's something just not right with her. I'm glad she's not here.*

I wondered where everyone else was, though. There should be at least a dozen more people here if this was a company announcement. And, where was Trevor?

I looked over at Gina. She held her hands in her lap, clasped together so tight her knuckles were white. *I guess she's as nervous as I am. What is this big announcement?*

Trevor hurried in. "Sorry for being late."

"No problem," said Bruce. "We're just getting started." He held his hand out to Trevor. "The podium is all yours."

Trevor smiled and glanced around at all of us. "First, I must apologize to those of you who I did not consult. *He's eyeing Gina and me, humph.* It was such a last minute find I hadn't time. As you know, we've been playing around with the idea of becoming a little less transparent in our operations. We deal with some high-value items and security is our main concern. Those of you who have been invited to this meeting are the core staff and I trust that you will all keep what is said here in strict confidence.

We will be moving our offices out of New York temporarily because security has become a major issue. I can't explain the details at this time. Just know that we have thought long and hard on this issue and moving is the best solution, for now."

Trevor took a sip of water and gazed at the group.

His eyes lingered on me just a little longer than on the others, sending heat to my cheeks.

He cleared his throat. "Some of our staff will remain here to continue working on the auction house. I'm sure you are all curious as to where we will be relocating." He glanced at me. "We have secured property in Scranton, Pennsylvania as a temporary location."

I nearly fell off my chair. *What the?* I shot a look at Gina. Her mouth was gaping open. I forced my attention back to Trevor.

"The property we have secured is a hundred-year-old church. It's been empty for some time and is in the process of renovation." He looked at me. "Egypt, do you have any information or advice about your area for our company?"

Holy crap, Mary, Mother of God, help us. I couldn't believe my ears. Our town we escaped from is too near Scranton. And now we were going back! I held in my screams and choked out a comment. "Well, if you are looking for anonymity, that's a good place for it. It's a pretty sleepy area." I couldn't say more or I would start shouting curse words. I took a deep breath. *Scranton? Maybe he thought I would be happier close to family. NOT! And Gina? She has been sooo happy away from her controlling family. Jesus H. Christ. We're trapped.*

Gina leaned over whispering to me, "Don't look so downhearted, Egypt. It won't be forever. He said, 'temporary'. If you don't lighten up, you'll get me depressed.

64

We'll get through this." She sighed. "Just remember, we're going to Rome—great eateries, good looking men, shopping, and sight-seeing. And men."

I felt better. "Yeah, let's concentrate on that." I still wasn't convinced that this move *would* be temporary but I resigned myself to riding it out. At least by tomorrow, we will be on a plane headed for Italy.

***

That night, while finishing up my packing, I tried *not* to bring up the subject of our move. Gina seemed to be doing okay, even though she was unusually quiet. After an hour of this, I couldn't stand it anymore. That's when Gina broke the silence.
"Egypt. Look at us, all quiet and reserved right before we're about to jet off to a beautiful country. I mean, we're going to Italy!" She dropped onto the bed. "We need to talk about the "S" bomb we were hit with today."

When I didn't respond, she tried again. "I'm not abandoning you over this, if that's your worry. I'm stickin' with you, pal."

She looked at me with pleading eyes. "I won't lie to you. I'm a little tense about going back." She shuddered. "Say something, please."

I was still in such a funk that when I opened my mouth to speak, nothing much came out.

"Never mind. We'll deal with this together, later. Okay?"

"Okay. I wanted to get away from our home town as if my life depended on it. Now we're stepping right back in. I'm afraid if my mother finds out I'm back, she'll badger me to death to come back home to 'grind'. I'd probably go comatose and cut off a finger! "

I paced the floor. Gina said nothing. "The only upside is that I'll be able to see Uncle Max and Grandpa. They are the only ones who ever understood me." I stopped and studied the ceiling. "Plus, there's our Eternal Treasures mystery. In due time, we *are* going to discover what's really going on. No matter where we live." The thought of that made me feel much better. Plus, however much my mother nagged, I wasn't a child anymore. I can just say 'no' to her.

Gina leaped over to me and smothered me in a big hug. "That's the Egypt I know and love—the dynamo with the fire that burns bright."

"Yeah. All that worked up an appetite. I'm ordering dinner. You want Chinese, or pizza?"

"Pizza is a sensitive subject." Gina made a frownie-face. "How about Chinese?"

"Great. Maybe my fortune cookie will have good news for us."

CHAPTER ELEVEN

Scranton, PA

Max relaxed in the easy chair, reading a new spy-thriller. He was enjoying a few days off and a chance to visit family. Just as he finished a chapter, his father stomped in looking gruff and ticked off.

"Look, Max. Don't screw this thing up again. I brought you into this and don't want to be held responsible for anything bad that might happen to you. This be a dangerous game."

Max had heard it all before. He just wanted to return to his book. "Yea Pop, you got me into this. How the—"

Pop ran his hand through his steel-grey hair. "You take over for me 'cause I think I finally be too old for this." He lowered himself into a chair.

"Pop. You're built like a tank. You've still got what it takes."

"Yeah. So *you say.*" He sighed. "And, what we do about Egypt?"

"What do you mean?"

He scowled. "When I find out Egypt and Gina work for Bruce and Trevor, I almost bust open and turn red like the devil. How did this happen?"

"I have no idea." Max put his book on the table next to his chair. "She might have just wanted a better life—reached for the brass ring. You know she's always thrived on adventure."

"Exciting, yes—this crazy, no!" Pop pounded the chair arms.

He was turning purple. Max was worried. "Take it Easy, Pop. Don't give yourself a stroke."

"Stroke, my ass. Now I *have* to get involved. My word, last word."

"Okay, okay. Have it your way Pop. Do whatever you want."
"What I want? I want Bruce's head on a plate. And you know I can do it. He'll regret he ever knew Stash Yagelska!"

Max went to him and put a hand on his dad's shoulder. "Hey. Don't think like that. It's not Bruce's fault. How did you get involved with them, anyway?"
He relaxed a little but Max still saw anger in his father's eyes. "It's no business of yours, hear me? Don't ask. When I'm ready, you will learn."
"I hear you, Pop. I won't ask again." *I still want to know. I'll find out, somehow.*

Pop sat back down on the chair. "You make sure my granddaughter safe—or someone will pay."

"I love her, too, you know." *God forbid he gets too involved in this mess. He can be a pain in the ass. He's headstrong and stubborn, just like Egypt. Must be where she gets it.*

***

Two days later, Stash Yagelska's plane landed in New York. Taking a cab to Eternal Treasures, stomping his huge feet into the door, bypassing Myrtle, and into Bruce's office he stormed. He kept demanding Trevor join them. Trevor arrived and sat on a chair in front of Bruce's desk.

"Mr. Yagelska," said Bruce. "Please come in."

"Don't you 'Mr. Yagelska,' me!" He marched up to Bruce. "I want to know how the hell you got my granddaughter and her friend, Gina involved in all this!"

Bruce looked stunned. "Well. She showed up here for an interview and we liked her."

Trevor stood and extended a hand toward the other chair. "Please. Have a seat."

After a moment of hesitation, Stash sat. "Well. I'm listening."

"We honestly didn't know she was your granddaughter when we hired her." said Trevor.

"You didn't do a background check? You check everyone from the janitor up!" yelled Stash.

Bruce leaned back in his chair. "We did a background check. Your name did *not* appear on the report. It wasn't until later that we discovered her relationship to you." He shuddered at the idea that Stash would find out.
Trevor added. "By then, she was doing such a good job, we couldn't fire her. She loves it here."

Stash leaned back, thinking about what they had said. *They're not telling me something. Play it close, old man.* He forced a smile. "Ah, well, what's done is done." He leaned forward and stared at Bruce. "If one hair on my granddaughter, or her friend's is harmed—well remember Tommy? I don't think he likes living in a wheel chair, do you?"

Bruce shivered. "I understand. We will give her protection first priority."

Stash stood and gave the two men an, I-mean-business look then turned and left the office like he owned those men. After hailing a cab, he told the driver to take him to The James

Hotel and pulled out his phone to call in some favors. *I'll get my girls the protection they need. Those yahoos couldn't protect a mouse from a cat. Bah!*

CHAPTER TWELVE

I gripped the arms of my seat as the plane seemed to crawl across the Atlantic Ocean. "Oh, Gina. Look at all that water below us. I think I'm going to be sick. I hate big, deep, cold bodies of water. If we go down, they'll never find us—just like Amelia Earhart." I started to panic. "First class is the worst place to be on a plane if it crashes."

"Egypt." Gina squeezed my hand. "Put on your eye mask and take some deep breaths. Relax. We'll be there soon."

She handed me the black-velvet mask. It should have been the 'real' Black Velvet. I stared at it.

"Okay. I will. But, only if I can have one of those pills you gave me on our way to California. If not that, how about a stiff whiskey?"

Gina sighed. "For such a smart girl, you sure are high maintenance at times. Well. I could use a drink myself. Relax. I'll see to it." She unbuckled and went to the flight attendant's station. I think she had to flee from me a few moments.

I closed my eyes and began to breathe in an even, rhythmic pattern.

"Egypt?"

I opened my eyes. Gina had returned and a flight attendant offered us two Jack Daniels on the rocks. She sipped hers. I downed mine in one gulp. Old Jack, he's good too.
A few minutes later, I felt much better. I wasn't much of a drinker and this one hit me like a Tsunami. *Next trip, I'll do much better. What a basket case. I'll sign up for some hypnosis sessions. I hear they work really well.* The plane hit

an air pocket. Instead of screaming, I tensed a little, and then I relaxed. *Thank you, Mr. Jack Daniels.*

Gina stared at me with a smirk. "You're drunk. And on one drink. I can't believe you're such a cheap date." She grinned and pointed to the eye mask. "Go to sleep."

***

After we deplaned, we had no trouble retrieving our luggage and clearing customs. I was surprised when they asked me not to open the briefcase I was carrying. *Maybe Bruce and Trevor pulled some strings.*

On our way out, there was a crowd of people holding up signs with names on them.

"There's us," said Gina heading for a young man with blond hair and a skimpy mustache.

His sign read "Egypt and Gina, E.T."
Somehow that pleased me. It really made us sound like an important team.

The sign-toting young man greeted us in Italian.

"Buongiorno."

Gina responded, *"Grazie. Ciao."*

I looked at him with a blank stare. "My Italian is a bit rusty. Do you speak English?"

He smiled. "Ah, Pardon, please, "Good morning. I am Angelo. I will be your escort. A car is waiting." He turned and signaled two men who appeared and helped us with our luggage. "This way." He led us through the crowd and out of the airport where a long black limo waited.

72

"Wow," I said under my breath.

When we stepped into the limo, there were two men already there. They introduced themselves as Antonio and Antonio.

This could get confusing. I heard Gina stifle a snigger.

"I'm Egypt." I turned to my friend. "This is Gina."
"Pleased to meet you," said Antonio #1. The other Antonio nodded.

Their blue eyes and sandy hair gave them away as northern Italians; very handsome indeed.

Neither offered any conversation on the way to the Babuino 181 hotel, so I leaned into the soft leather seat and watched the scenery fly by. Gina had closed her eyes. I thought, again, of our unbroken code and how it fit into the mysterious web of intrigue surrounding Eternal Treasures. The lure of continuing our investigation tugged at my sleeve. At this point, though, it seemed hopeless, so I stashed it in the back of my mind, determined to enjoy Rome.

At the hotel, both Antonios accompanied us inside to make sure there was no problem with registration. It all went as smooth as a baby's bottom.

"Here's our card," said Antonio #1. "Whenever you are ready for some sightseeing, call us."

"Thank you." I slipped the card into my pocket.

They turned and left, and we headed for the elevator.

Entering our suite, I let out a low whistle. "The title 'suite' is an understatement. I wonder if this is where royalty stays when they're in town." *I do love the word 'sweet.'*

Gina, who was no stranger to luxury, looked dumbstruck. "Wow."

I sat on the beautiful sofa. "Ah, thank you great goddess Isis for watching and bearing us treasures and excesses."

Gina kicked off her boots and dropped down beside me. "Now, *this* is luxury I could get used to." She jumped up, flinging her arms out wide and twirling until she fell onto the floor. "My parents always made me feel guilty about enjoying wonderful things. They are sooo conservative."

"I totally understand. But," I said lowering onto the floor near her. "We need to stay focused on our mission. I make the delivery tomorrow. Hopefully, this time, we *won't* be followed."

Gina gave me a mock salute. "I'm at your service. Hey. I have an idea. After you give the package to Mr. Alberti, we could stake out his place. Watch for him to go to the cultural ministry. It's only about five blocks from his office—I looked at the map while you slept on the plane. I'll bet he walks the item over around noon. If it gets there safely, fine. If there's trouble, we'll be there to help."

She grinned like a kid.

"Great idea, but how could we help?"

"Well, I do have a little secret," said Gina.

"Okay, I'll bite. What secret?"

"Do you remember the eighth grade when I gained all that weight and everyone made fun of me?"

"Sure. But what does that have to do with our mission?"

"One day, Wart and Tommy jumped me, scaring me half to death. They called me names and taunted me until I cried."

"I remember, but. . ."

"Well—confession time—it was pizza that made me so fat. I couldn't get enough of it. Now I can't stand the sight of it."

"Gina, will you get to the point, please?"

"Okay, okay. Well, because of those boys, I vowed never to be without protection. So now I always carry a knife—sometimes in my boot." She let out a sigh. "Now you know." She patted her bare ankle. "I'll have to buy a new one here. The one I have is too old and might break." She got up and rifled through the ornate desk by the window. "Aha!" she exclaimed. "This will have to do in the meantime." She held up a sturdy letter opener." She walked over to the sofa where she had taken off her boots and slipped it into a sheath on the inside.

"Wow! A knife. Good choice of weapon. I always wondered why you guarded your boots like a watchdog. I carry a gun, sometimes. I called your cousin, Vincent. He got it for me."

Gina's jaw dropped. "A gun? You?"

"Yeah, I didn't tell you because I didn't want to scare you. And, it's only a stun gun."

"How did you get it past airport security?"

"It's a special plastic." I saw the look of horror on her face. "I have a permit. It's entirely legal. Well, mostly, anyway. I put it in checked luggage just in case."

"Egypt. You didn't have to keep it a secret. I would have called Vincent for you. Though I'm afraid, you know my uncle has ears and eyes everywhere. He is so damn protective.

Kind of like your uncle and grandfather. And, as soon as possible we'll be getting you a pocket in your boot to slip it into."

"Let's just hope this doesn't get back to him," I said. "And don't remind me of my protectors either. Hey, let's change the subject. Remember the conversations I overheard and the recording I was slipped with Bruce and Trevor talking about a 'big project'?"

Gina nodded.

"Well, I have gut feeling that Eternal Treasures has gotten itself mixed up with some pretty unsavory people. Their project must be really beaucoup important for them to go to such extremes."

"I'm sure we'll get answers if we just keep digging." Gina got to her feet. "I'm going to unpack and take a bubble bath."

She sauntered off to the bathroom.

***

The next morning, I called for room service for breakfast. I must have ordered everything on the menu. We stuffed ourselves.

After breakfast we dressed—casual but chic. I grasped the handle of the briefcase that contained the artifact. I tried not to think about how important it was to get this little treasure to its destination.

"Gina, your Italian is better than mine. Would you call the front desk and order a taxi?"

"Va bene." She grinned.

While she was on the phone, I started itching to know what I would be delivering. I wasn't told what was in the briefcase and not knowing was driving me mad. I wanted to peek at history.

Gina cradled the phone. "The taxi will be here in five minutes."

"Thanks. I'm going to take a look at what we're carrying."

"I think that's a really bad idea." Gina frowned.

"Oh, come on. I'll put it back exactly the way it was." My fingers were already unlocking the heavy case and lifting the foam covering the artifact. I took it out carefully. "It's a Roman bas relief of men on chariots. This is probably 3rd century—a depiction of a chariot race in the Circus Maximus. Some of the horses are missing. It's beautiful."

"Just looks like a little piece of plaster with pictures, to me," said Gina with a sigh.

"It's amazing and priceless."

Gina shrugged. "If you say so. I love horses, even if they don't love me."

I carefully recovered the relief and locked the briefcase, hoping that Mr. Alberti wouldn't be able to tell that I had taken a look.

Outside the hotel, our taxi was waiting. I gripped the briefcase like it was carrying a transplant organ. Gina gave the driver the address and he took off like a jet.

A few minutes later we arrived at Mr. Alberti's office. I paid the fare then we turned and faced a rather modest but modern building. Inside I was relieved that the receptionist spoke decent English.

"We're here to see Mr. Alberti." I handed her my card. "I believe he is expecting me."

The Receptionist studied the card. Her eyes lit up. "Oh, *si*. Come right this way."

She picked up the intercom and said something in Italian.

"Go right in." She pointed to the office on the left.

I opened the double-doors. Gina walked in behind me. His office was large but not pretentious. Seated behind an impressive wooden desk, he looked to be about fifty or so, dressed in a finely tailored suit and expensive-looking silk tie. He's balding and rotund, but with nice features. Worry lines etched his face.

He must be married with children. He's wearing a wedding ring. I glanced at the wall and saw a framed photo of him with what I assumed was his family. *I thought he probably had at least three daughters, and a son. I guess I was right. Fathers lose hair over daughters.*

I extended my hand. "Mr. Alberti, I'm Egypt." I turned to Gina. "This is Gina. I have a delivery for you."

He rounded his desk. His big smile lit up his face. "Please. Call me Luigi." He greeted us with very European kisses on our cheeks. We settled into soft chairs. He offered us cappuccino.

"How kind of you," said Gina.

He stepped over to his desk, touched the com then ordered cappuccino for three.
As we sipped, Luigi seemed intent on just relaxing and chatting for a while.

"I insist on taking you both out to dinner tonight—with my wife, of course. I want to show you the authentic Italy."

"That would be wonderful." I looked to Gina. She smiled. "We accept."

He clapped his hands together. "Fine. We will come for you at eight this evening." Glancing at the briefcase, he added, "Now I think you have something for me?"

"Oh, yes. Sorry." I handed him the case.

He accepted it with such obvious joy, it warmed my heart.

"I will take it to the ministry today." He ran his hand across the case as if *it* was the actual artifact. "I can't wait for us to gloat over this."

CHAPTER THIRTEEN

After leaving Luigi's office, I pulled Gina aside. "Let's wait around the corner of the building. He should be leaving for the ministry any minute."

Gina puckered her lips. "Do Italians eat lunch at the same time as Americans?"

"Well, no, actually. I didn't think about that. But he was so excited, I'll bet we don't have long to wait, no matter what traditional lunch time is."

"Okay. We wait, then."

"*Shhhh. Here he comes.*" I tugged her further back into the shadow of the building. "Let's let him get a block ahead of us so he won't see us following." I peeked around the corner of the building. "Okay. Let's go."

As we watched Luigi jauntily walking along, briefcase in hand, I spotted two men who seemed to be following him at close range. We picked up our pace. My hand went to the stun gun in my pocket, ready to pull it out and use it if needed.

Before we could get close enough to warn him, the men grabbed Luigi's arms and yanked them behind his back. Then quick as lightning, one of them pulled out a gun and rammed it into his back.

"What do we do now?" Gina whispered to me. *Thanks for the shooting lessons and all those self-defense classes, Uncle Max. I may need them today.* "Gina. Follow my lead." She nodded.

I hurried closer to one of the men. Remembering my karate training, I managed a near-crippling kick to his back. He lurched forward and dropped his gun. Gina ran to grab it. While he was trying to catch his breath, I pulled out my weapon and stunned him. He toppled to the sidewalk like a boulder over a cliff.

When I looked up, the other guy had Gina in a choke hold. Luigi was out cold on the walk. *No blood. He's probably okay.* "Gina, the boot!" I yelled. Understanding filled her eyes. In an instant, she elbowed the guy, twisted and almost faster than I could see, had the letter opener out of her boot and landed a nasty stab to his thigh.

He screamed and ran away, leaving a trail of blood down the street.

I was feeling good about what we did before I looked over at the guy I grappled with. He was gone. It was then I noticed the crowd starting to gather but I had no time to explain. I ran to Luigi who was starting to come to, holding his head. Miraculously, the briefcase was still securely locked to his wrist.

"What happened?" He looked at us in disbelief.
I explained that we had thwarted would-be thieves.

He stood up and brushed off his suit. "Thank you, both! If it wasn't for you, I might have lost the artifact, or worse, my life."

"We're just glad you're okay," I said furtively glancing around to make sure the thieves were not lurking somewhere. "You'd better hurry." I saw that the crowd had disbursed— the excitement was over.

Luigi stood, brushed off his slacks, and nodded to us then hurried on his way.

As Gina and I walked to the nearest taxi stand, I was fuming. "Why didn't Bruce provide Luigi with some security? We could all have been killed."

"Yeah," said Gina. "And just look at my outfit. It's practically ruined. That guy spurted blood on it and the other guy ripped my sleeve!" She was furious. "I don't know why I didn't think of the letter opener. I was scared, I guess. Thanks for the prompt."

"Let's just hope we don't need it again." I linked arms with her and we flagged a taxi at the stand.
On the way to the hotel, I was still ranting. "I'll bet those men worked for Cryptonomics. I'm going to find out for sure. And, I will let Bruce and Trevor know how I feel about their lax security or poor planning. Someone knew about this drop. Jeesh!"

"Oh, goody. Another adventure," said Gina.

I wasn't sure if she was serious or being sarcastic.

"Oh, no," groaned Gina. "One of my nails broke."

"Gina. Nails can be fixed. You can get it pampered when we get back to the hotel."

"I know. You probably think I'm being a baby. But I need some time to process what just happened."

***

Gina returned from the hotel day-spa all polished and beautiful. "I feel so much better. Now, what shall I wear tonight?" She took in a breath. "Do you think Luigi and his wife will still take us to dinner?"

"He hasn't called to cancel, so I say we get gussied up and be ready."

We spent the next two hours dressing and promptly at eight, we received a call from the front desk letting us know that Mr. Alberti was here.

We grabbed our bags and hurried to the elevator.
He welcomed us with open arms and ushered us to his limo.

"Egypt, Gina. This is my wife, Sophia."

She extended a hand. "It is so good to meet you both. Luigi tells me you came to his rescue today." She patted her heart. "I don't know how to thank you."

"No thanks are needed," I said. "It's good to meet you, too."

Luigi rubbed his hands together. I'll bet you've never tasted *real* Italian pizza. You are in for a treat!"

The Limo pulled up in front of the Pizzeria Remo. It looked unassuming but I held off judgment.
The driver opened our doors and we walked toward the restaurant. The minute we entered, the heavenly aroma hit my nose. *Oh my god, that smells good.* I knew, even before tasting that I was in for a life altering experience.

At the table, Luigi ordered wine. The waiter seemed to know our host. Luigi introduced us in Italian. Gina chatted with him for a few seconds.

Show off. I smiled internally. *I should have paid more attention to learning Italian than ancient Egyptian and Latin.*

Luigi ordered for us by filling out a paper menu on the table. The server nodded and rushed to the kitchen.

A few minutes later, we were served *Suppli*—a fried roll stuffed with rice and ragu meat. "Good lord, this is amazing," I blurted out.

Luigi and Sophia grinned ear to ear.

Next in line was *bruschetta*, bursting with flavor. I'd never tasted bread that good.

When the pizzas arrived, we were on our second bottle of wine. I was feeling no pain. I noticed that most customers were using the serve-yourself-wine. I guess Luigi was special to have bottles brought to the table.

We had the *Margherita con Bufala* pizza and a *Diavola*. "Mmmm," was all I could comment.

Being polite, Gina indulged with a few bites claiming she was already full. The thin crust is blistered and slightly charred from the wood-fired pizza oven. This was a mind-blowing food experience.

"How is it possible for this to be so much better than any pizza in America?" asked Gina.
Sophia seemed more than eager to answer. "It's the minerals in the water they use to make the bread. The yeast is a very old strain. There is a type of hardwood charcoal, and the sun-ripened tomatoes are exquisite. These kinds of ingredients are not readily available in America."

I said little the rest of the night. I kept recollecting that scrumptious meal, and the good company.

CHAPTER FOURTEEN

A meeting at Eternal Treasures, New York. While Egypt and Gina were in Italy.

Outside the window at Eternal Treasures, rain fell in sheets onto the streets below. Inside the meeting room, Bruce and Max discussed the ramifications of Egypt being employed at the company.

"Bruce," said Max tapping his fingers on his knees "Is it true that Egypt is working for Eternal Treasures?"

Bruce tightened his lips. This wasn't a conversation he wanted to have.

Max gave an exasperated sigh. "What the —?" What am I going to do if she and Gina find out about my involvement? This makes me very unhappy." He clucked his tongue and stared into Bruce's eyes.

"Now, Max. It'll be fine. How could they find out?" He turned to face the window, staring at the water rivulets on the window. Raking his hands through his hair, he blew out a breath. "Oh, cripes." Turning back, he rounded his desk and leaned on the edge. "Max. If it weren't for you and your men, there would be no rewards for us and no antiquities returned. Crypto has no ethics and their business model is governed by greed. It's a race to see who can raise the most money to begin the project and still keep it secret. We are a small band of dedicated men and women compared to Crypto's far reach." He studied Max to gauge his reaction.

Max extended a hand, palm up. "Continue."
"Remember," Bruce said after sipping coffee,' it's over for us if they win. And worse if they find out how much we're bluffing, the only option for us would be to fold our cards and scatter them to the heavens for help."

"I understand, Bruce. We're playing a tight game and anything's possible. Egypt could find out through someone's mistake, slip of the tongue, or a careless file left unlocked." He leaned forward. "Even with this hanging over me, I haven't lost sight of the real goal. It's important to beat that other company." He pushed out of the chair and stood within inches of Bruce. "There must be no harm to these girls. Crypto is dangerous. So far, we've convinced them that we know everything. I know this because they still allow you to keep going in hopes of leading them to the weapon." He stepped back and eased into the chair.

Bruce swallowed hard just as Trevor joined them. "Come in. We were discussing the Egypt and Gina situation."

Trevor nodded, shook hands with Max and took a seat.

Bruce continued. "Max. They are watching our every step and believe that we will lead them to the site. They plan to get the jump on us and leave us scattered in the dust. It's dangerous for everyone. They specialize in chaos, murder, and knives in the dark. Our plan is to mislead and leave when we know the desired outcome is absolute."

Trevor lifted a finger, "May I interject?" He didn't wait for an answer. "Max, I don't think Egypt will find out. You're working opposite ends of the project. You're operation is run from this office and we're moving Egypt and Gina to the Scranton division for now."

"You're what?" hissed Max. "You can't be serious. Tell me that's a joke. I can't believe what I'm hearing."

"Bruce held up his hands, "Boys! Calm down. Max. The girls have no knowledge of how we get our artifacts. They think it's through auctions—some of them are. They haven't questioned anything. Trust me. It'll be okay."

"Yeah, like I trusted you with the guys who turned out to be Albanian mobsters and nearly got us killed." Max rubbed the stubble on his chin and stared out the window.

Bruce shook his head. "I admit we've made some wrong moves. We aren't pros when it comes to mobster tactics. It seems as if there is an inside man. They seemed to know our plans before we did. That leak was plugged when we caught the new guy in the act, though. Things have been going better of late, but certainly not perfect. We have to keep going, even though Crypto wants us out of the way or dead." Bruce refilled his coffee. "We've also been working with some of the greatest and most knowledgeable archaeologists and Egyptologists alive today. Permits take time in Egypt and depend on who you know; they can make all the difference. Dr. Hawassi has been invaluable."

Bruce thought he should talk privately with Trevor after Max left about keeping his relationship with Egypt a secret. Bruce always had eyes in the back of his head. *It wouldn't be good for Max Yagelska or Grandpa to find out. I'd better warn Trevor to keep it quiet.*

CHAPTER FIFTEEN

Rome, the day after Egypt and Gina saved Luigi's life.

Gina and I decided that after our ordeal, we needed some
R&R so I called the Antonios to accept their offer for some
sightseeing. They asked us to pack overnight bags. They
wouldn't say why but we thought it sounded like a great
adventure.

When we met them in the lobby, I did a double-take. They
looked like models straight out of GQ. Both dressed in pricey
jeans, expensive-tailored shirts under cashmere sweater-
vests.

We gussied up for the day, too. Gina donned her designer
jeans and powder-blue cashmere sweater. Her tasteful but
obviously expensive jewelry sparkled. And, of course she
wore her ostrich leather boots.

I wasn't quite as elegant, but did well, I think. My cashmere
top was pink, as were my Ferragamo shoes.

"Good morning, Egypt, Gina. Ready?" Antonio #1 smiled,
revealing dimples and perfect teeth. "The car is just outside."

After we were settled into the limo, Antonio #2 asked, "I hope
you will enjoy Tuscany. It is one of the most beautiful regions
in Italy."

"Oh," said Gina. I've always wanted to go there. How
exciting!" She turned to me and gave me that secret eye look
we share that meant we were about to have a "very" fun
time.
As everyone chatted and enjoyed the ride, I had to push
memories of what happened to Luigi to the back of my mind.
I vowed to give Bruce a face-to-face rant when we got back
to New York.

Focusing on the landscape rushing by, I marveled at how beautiful it was on this glorious day.

When we reached our destination and filed out of the limo, the cool breeze refreshed the air. The sun shone bright in the clear azure sky.

"Where are we," I asked, looking around at an amazing landscape devoid of buildings.

"Ah!" said Antonio #2. We are in Tuscany. This is where we will have our luncheon." He signaled the driver who retrieved a large hamper and blanket from the trunk.

"This way." Antonio #1 began to climb a low, green hill.

At the top the vista of a charming medieval city spread out before us. It was breathtaking.

The driver spread the blanket and set the hamper onto the ground. He tipped his hat. "Enjoy." I watched him head back down the hill. *In America, he would have been invited to join us. Well, 'When in Rome. . .'*

"Where is this?" I asked.

Antonio #2 smiled. "This is Cortona in the Tuscany province" He gazed at the spread of red-tiled roofs. "Not far from the more famous Florence."
I glanced at Gina who seemed far more interested in her wine than in the scenery.

Antonio #2 extended his hand toward the town. "In the 600's it was conquered by the Etruscans but eventually became a Romany colony. Then in the 13th century it was ruled by a powerful family, then by the Medici. My mother was born here."

After consuming two bottles of wine, almost a whole wheel of cheese, fresh fruit, and rustic crackers, we were headed back down the hill to the limo.

The driver took the blanket and hamper from Antonio #1, stowed them, then opened the door for us.

"Ladies, now you will see Roma. Not the Roma of tourists but we will show you the Antonios' Roma." He grinned and winked at us as we left.

We strolled through Roman ruins and were entertained with little-known stories of their history. I was in my element. I looked at Gina and surmised that she wasn't quite as enthralled as I was about fallen treasures. I waved the boys ahead. "We'll catch up." When they were out of earshot, I asked, "Okay, Gina. Are you bored, or what?"

She shrugged. "Well, it's okay but they remind me of demolished apartment buildings destroyed to make way for new construction. Sort of like what my uncle sometimes does."

We walked arm in arm toward the Antonios. Gina stopped and looked around. "I was wondering, though, what kind of people built these structures. They are pretty impressive for being so old."

"Ladies," said Antonio #1, taking Gina's arm. "Are you tired?"

"Oh, no!" said Gina, obviously more interested now that Antonio showed personal interest in her."

I gave her a wink. Antonio #2 came to me and took my arm in his. "Call me Tony?"

I nearly fainted as thoughts of Trevor evaporated like fog in the sunshine.

After visiting every site in Rome, I was tired. My feet hurt and my back was starting to ache. I was relieved when Tony said we were going back to Tuscany, but this time to Florence—by private plane.

I knew Gina was relieved. Ruins aren't exactly her thing. She was thinking about shopping. In fact, so was I.

After we had landed and transferred ourselves to the waiting car, Gina put on her most winning smile. "Tony, Antonio, I'd love to get some shopping in. Do you mind?"

"Not at all!" said Tony. "Lead the way."

I was relieved. *Nice. Not usually a man thing. At least in the good ol' US of A.*
Three shops later, I glanced at Tony. He seemed to be having a good time. He must have read my mind.

"Ah, Egypt. It has been a long time since I've enjoyed my own Italia so much. I love seeing your pretty blue eyes open with wonder at my country—ruins, medieval towns *and* shops."

"I noticed that you knew quite a bit about ancient Italy."

He grinned. "Perhaps that's because I am an archaeologist."

This was really good news. Handsome, charming *and* educated in my passion for the past. "My mother has an interest in the ancient world, too. She's a bit, shall I say, unusual. That's why I was named Egypt. She's the reason I chose archaeology as my major in college."

Antonio came up to us. "I agree. It is good to see happy faces.

***

"I hate to admit it, but I'm really tired. I think I'm done shopping for now." I blew out a breath and glanced at Gina.

"Well, I'm getting hungry."

Everyone agreed that it was time to stop and have something to eat.

We headed for the airport and boarded the plane that brought us to Florence. I immediately removed my shoes and leaned back into the seat.
"We will have our meal at my uncle's vineyard," said Antonio.

The plane flew over the most breathtaking landscape. We landed on a private airstrip outside of acres of grapevines surrounding an enormous estate.

"After our meal, we can go into town to shop for jewelry. This is the hub of the Etruscan district. They create the most intricate gold ornaments. Some artists specialize in recreating the ancient pieces. There is also the famous Uffizi Museum.

"This is beautiful beyond words, Antonio." I shaded my eyes and gazed over the hillsides.

"Yes, I try to spend my free time here. One day, I will own my own vineyard."

"I love it here and stay as long as I can each time," said Tony. "I'm glad you like it." He gazed deep into my eyes.

Images of Tony and me rolling around on a giant antique bed with snow-white sheets floated through my mind. *Stop it, Egypt. Pay attention to what he's saying. Focus, Grasshopper. Focus.*

"They are coming," said Antonio, pointing to a car in the distance, bumping over the road and kicking up a cloud of dust behind.

The car skidded to a stop and a middle-aged man with sandy, curly hair and bright eyes leapt from the car, arms wide. *"Buongiorno!"*

He hugged everyone then ushered us into the car.

At the estate, long trestle tables were set up, groaning with food. Women rushed around in preparation for the guests. Kisses and hugs were as numerous as fireflies on a summer night. I truly felt welcome.

The food was amazing. The wine was superb. Tony couldn't keep his eyes off of me.

A couple of hours later, with candle lanterns lit, talk continued to be lively. I stifled a yawn.

Tony and Antonio stood and announced that it was time for us to be leaving. More kisses. More hugs. Regrets expressed.

In the car, I caught Gina nodding off. When she woke up and she saw me looking at her, she whispered, "Too much food and wine. It was wonderful."
That night we stayed in a beautiful hotel. Shopping and the museum would wait until the next day.
The last couple of days had been so wonderful, I had almost forgotten about Bruce and his incompetence putting Luigi in such danger. I decided to keep it in the back of my mind—for now and vowed to just enjoy myself.
After lunch, Gina and I decided we needed a little down time so we could party hardy that night with Antonio and Tony.
We went back to our room and treated ourselves to rest and planning what we would wear that night.

The guys were meeting us in the lobby at eight. When that time arrived, we took a last look in the mirror. "Yes!" I said. "We are smokin' hot. I can hear the sizzle."

I knew that our efforts had paid off when I saw the look in the men's eyes. I was radiant in red. Gina oozed glamour in jade.

We had reservations in the hotel's finest restaurant where we were treated like royalty, and ate ourselves silly.

"That *porketta* was fantastic!" I said. "It oozed flavor."

Tony beamed. "The meal was wonderful. I'm so glad you liked it. Gelato?"

"Of course," said Gina with enthusiasm.

I'd never seen her enjoy food so much. She was usually overly concerned with calories.

I was studying Tony when he quipped, "What are you staring at? Do I have gelato on my chin?"

"I'm sorry. I was just thinking that you look so much like someone from Northern Italy. Your lovely eyes carry a bit of mystery in them."

"Ah, you know your characteristics, I see. Thank you, Egypt." He beamed. "Shall we?"

Tony escorted me out while Gina and Antonio lingered over a glass of wine.

"Would you like to come to my room?" Tony said with a little hesitation.

Would I? Does the Pope wear funny hats? "That would be nice."

Once inside, Tony stood close behind me and whispered in my ear, "I had such a terrific time with you today."

Well, that and the closeness of his hard body curled my toes. I had to catch my breath. When I turned toward him, I started trembling a bit and a rush of scorching heat raced through me.

Tony smiled. "The sparks between us are burning me, Egypt."

"Oh, I like how you talk. Let's burn the fire together." Sparks quickly erupted into bonfire.

He put his arms around my waist and drew me to him and he ran his lips over my face then held my head and kissed me, long and deep. I was intoxicated with desire.

Piece by piece our clothes dropped or tossed throughout the room. He picked me up and carried me into the bedroom.

He laid me onto the bed and traced his luscious lips all over me, up and down. I moaned with pleasure.

In an erotic dance, we churned and turned over and over in the huge bed. Then, without warning, he stopped. He looked into my eyes, brushed a tendril of hair away from my face and gently ran his fingers over my thighs. His touch felt like silk.

"It seems your passion matches mine," he said. "I can see it in your eyes."

He kissed me and we made love with abandon and gusto. It was as if I had entered an alternate universe where nothing but pleasure and enchantment existed.
When we had both expended ourselves, he lifted off of me and lay on his back, panting. Turning his head to me, he smiled. "Egypt, that was beyond anything."

I turned to face him. "Tony. This is the Italy I will never forget."

"Come," he said as he leapt off the bed. Taking my hand, he repeated, "Come with me." He led me to the balcony and we gazed at the bejeweled night sky. Then he wrapped me in a blanket and held me close.

Back inside, he handed me a silk robe. I padded into the bathroom to shower and do something with the wild mane my hair had become. When I came out he was dressed in pajama bottoms and had opened a bottle of champagne. "To the most beautiful American woman in the universe," he said, holding the flute high.

I wondered if Gina had an equally wonderful evening. *I'll bet she did.*

Tony and I talked until near dawn then I kissed him, dressed and said my goodbye.
He held me close and whispered. "I shall dream of you."

Closing the door softly behind me, I sighed. *Wow.*

***

With our night with the Antonios, fresh with memories, our minds would remain in Rome for a while, even when packing our bags for home. As magical as my time with Tony was, I knew in my heart that Trevor was still the man for me.

In the hotel lobby, Tony said with sadness in his voice, "Alas, our trip is over and we return to the boring routine once more."
"Yes," added Antonio. "We will miss you both." He said "both" but he was looking at Gina.

96

Now that the Disney-esque glitter had cleared from my brain, I was thinking again about the danger that Luigi was subjected to, thanks to Bruce. We had told the Antonios about our harrowing experience.

As reading my mind, Antonio said, "Please remember to tell your boss what happened to your friend. You were in as much danger as he."

I suddenly wanted to know what was really going on. "Who are you, really?" I asked looking from Tony to Antonio. "Are you connected with Eternal Treasures? And if so, in what way?"

Gina chimed in. "Yes. What is the truth?" She gave him the tell-me-or-else glare.

Tony and Antonio glanced at each other. "We can only say that we are Eternal Treasures liaisons. We cannot say more. I'm sorry."

Tony glanced toward the front glass doors. "It looks as if your taxi is here. Regrettably, I must say *ciao*. Please come back one day." He kissed me on the cheek then whispered. "Be careful. You never know where danger lies."

Antonio kissed Gina's hand and said something to her that I couldn't hear.

We wheeled our bags out of the hotel and climbed into the taxi, thinking of home.

On the way to the airport, I thought about what Tony had said to me. *What did he mean about danger? Does he know something we don't?*

CHAPTER SIXTEEN

New York, Eternal Treasures secrets

Ted frowned. He was worried. "Max. How do we know for sure they have the stolen goods from Egypt?"

"Because Bruce said so." Max made an exasperated sound. "Are *you* positive you disabled their security system?"

"Piece of cake, Max. It isn't even an up-to-date system. Stash would be proud. You'd think with all that treasure, they'd be a little more cutting-edge with their technology."

"Yo. Ted," said Sam, a member of Max's team. "Remember, only the Egyptian papyri—that's all." He shrugged his shoulders. I know you're always tempted when you see a delicious piece of art, but that's not what we're here for. Bruce and Trevor might hang you if you pulled a personal piece."

"Cripes," sounded Max. "Will you guys settle down and let Sam do his job?" *How did Bruce find these Cretins anyway? Or, was it Pop who found them?*

Max surveyed the team. "Ted. You be lookout. The piece is hidden somewhere where it won't be exposed to heat or dampness. Think for yourself."

Ted saluted, "My pleasure."

"Sam. If I learned anything as a cop, I'm sure we'll find what we're looking for. Sam, safes are your specialty. Start there. I'll look in other places." Max frowned and cracked his knuckles. "It just frosts my big Polish ass that people steal artifacts from other countries. What if some dizzy asshole tried to take our Constitution? Real dick heads."

Max stood. "Everyone know their job? Let's go!"

***

Max was the one who found the papyrus. It was wrapped in linen in a locked liquor cabinet. At least it *was* locked before Max Yagelska used his magic hands.

"Isn't it rich," said Max with venom in his voice, "that this pervert thief of special foreign property can't even be reported to the cops?"

"Yeah," Ted agreed. "But think of how mad they'll be when they discover *we* have it now. And, they *will* discover it. That mob has eyes like a potato."

"Maybe no one will find out it was us. The rich and powerful aren't always so smart," said Sam. "Besides, they can't report it, ha."
Max groaned. "All I know is that I don't want my niece and her friend to find out what I'm doing. I'm not sure what she does for the company but I'm glad she's not in this part of it. Too dangerous. Anyway, Bruce tells me she's perfectly safe. I hope he's right."

CHAPTER SEVENTEEN

The day we got back from Italy, I pushed aside my jet lag and made a bee line to Bruce's office. Sparrow tried to get in my way but I summarily pushed her aside and burst through his door. He looked up, obviously dazed to see me. I was fuming and without compunction.

"Egypt. What is it? You look really upset." Bruce put his pen down and studied me.

"You bet I'm upset. Someone could have been killed! It could have been me, Gina, or poor Luigi. Those mob thugs meant business. If it hadn't been for our quick thinking, they would have probably chopped Luigi's wrist off for the briefcase!"

"Egypt. Slow down. What are you talking about?" Bruce rounded his desk and indicated that we sit on the sofa.

I spilled the details of Luigi's attack and our defense of him. "I don't care if you fire me for yelling about this. I think there is a leak in the company. Somewhere in our offices is a spy that'd better be found before Gina or I do, or there will be much pain to pay for you both!"

"Egypt. I believe you. I'll look into it." He enthusiastically apologized.

"An apology won't do. We need better intelligence and security. Gina and I acting as tourists to detract attention didn't work. I want to know why this happened. Find a solution—fast! I'm sorry if I'm being belligerent, but Gina and I are fed up right now."
Just then Gina came rushing through the door. "I could hear you shouting all the way into the hall." She looked at Bruce. What the heck is this crap that we have to save everyone's ass, including our own? We want answers."

Bruce stood and indicated for Gina to sit. "I didn't mean for it to go this way. I thought it was a safe and innocuous way to handle it. We are trying to prevent them from stealing our future." He stuttered and didn't finish that thought. Running his fingers through his hair in obvious frustration, he pulled up a chair. "You're right. You deserve an explanation. We are having problems on two fronts. Perhaps it's time you know the 'whole' story."

This was more like it. I already knew more than he thought I did but I wasn't talking.

"Well, it's about time," said Gina.

"We didn't know about the antiquity problem until Italy. Trevor and I—thought the L.A. incident was just a thug looking to steal. But, now we aren't so sure. So, until this is resolved, you and Gina will be assigned only to ultra-safe assignments."

"How are you going to resolve it?" I asked.
"I have my resources," said Bruce rather cryptically.

"No way," said Gina. "We're in this too, and we will do some of our own sleuthing."

"Gina's right," I said. I'm not sitting on my ass forever because of this."
Bruce's eyes implored us to reconsider. "I feel responsible. The last thing I want is for either of you to be harmed. I can't allow you to be battered."

"Too late," Gina sat up straight and jutted out her stubborn chin. "We're in."

"I understand, but there's something else. I didn't want you to find out yet, but I see it can't be hidden anymore."

"Well?" I said, with a big question mark lighting up my face like a disco ball.

"It's the Russian mob. For some reason, they believe we've moved into their drug territory. We haven't."

He scanned our faces to see if we believed him. We did. Or at least *I* did. I'd have to ask Gina, later.

"We're legit. They don't want to hear it and are trying to even the score. We're not sure where they got such an idea, unless—. Never mind that now. That's one reason we all have to be careful. I have a man on it now. He's the best and will get to the bottom of this." He sat back in the chair, obviously relieved to have this out in the open. "So tread lightly for now."

Oh, crap. First Italy, now the mob? If I had balls, they'd be twisted so tight they'd be ready to fall off.

After we left Bruce's office, I grumbled to Gina. "I know he's not telling us everything. This whole thing better be resolved soon. If not, we could be dead meat on a stick with an apple on top." I groaned.

***

The next day I made sure to arrive at work early. I wanted to think about Bruce, Trevor, and the company. I thought I was the only one there, so when I heard a low voice around the corner coming from the reception desk, I froze. It was Bun Babe on her cell phone. I leaned in to eavesdrop.

She was speaking a language I didn't recognize. It's a good thing I have a phenomenal memory. Some of the words stuck in my brain for later. Then she said something in English—I heard my name and Gina's being mentioned.

This was a bit scary. I tiptoed back to my office and locked the door. Hurrying to my desk, I jotted down the foreign words as best I could. That done, I tiptoed quietly around the back entrance, then whistled and chirped through the front door, acting as if I had just arrived. As I passed her I gave her a big smile. *Bun Bitch.*

That evening, I told Gina about what I heard and showed her the list of words I wrote down. "Right from the mouth of the person I suspect might be the leak. But I couldn't find this language anywhere on the Internet. Perhaps I had it spelled wrong."

"I can go to the university language department. Someone there might be able to help." Gina grinned at her ingenuity and resourcefulness.
"Thanks pal. I really appreciate it."

She saluted. "At your service, Sarge." She turned and bounded out the door, list in hand.

"I'll be back at the apartment for lunch when you are through. I need to think and rest after all of this 'Craptonomic' stuff."

Two hours later, Gina rushed through the door. "Bingo! Let's hear it for me!"

"What, what?" I badgered. "Spill!"

"Yep. This Bun Bitch must be the leak," Gina said, head in the air and looking like she felt mighty good about herself. "According to the university head, she was telling the 'enemy' about our next excursion." She plopped down on the sofa. "Phew. I'm glad our itinerary was changed."

"Amen to that. I wonder who she's working for. Did you find out what the language is?"

"I sure did. From what he could tell from your phonetic spelling, it is probably Albanian." Gina handed me the list—a little crumpled, but still intact.

"Oh, God!" I hope she's their only spy. If it's Albanian, she's probably working for Cryptonomics." My stomach did quavering leaps. "They'll do anything to stymie our company."

Gina tapped my knee. "I'm sure she will be caught. We should tell Bruce right away, though."

"I'll tell him first thing in the morning."
"Great. For now, I think we need a drink." She left for the kitchen. I heard the pop of a champagne cork. She returned carrying the bottle and two glasses.

"Here's to Egypt and Gina!" *Clink.*

"Salute!" I called, then "Nas drovnja!"
After the bottle was consumed, I leaned back. "Gina, maybe we should go to church on Sunday. It couldn't hurt to get a little prayer in that this thing gets resolved without anyone getting hurt."

"Amen to that, my friend." Gina downed the last drops from her glass. "We need a little heavenly intervention. We may even get a statue to shed a tear for us." Then she cackled.

I had a brilliant idea. "Gina. What if we bugged Bun Bitch's desk then take the recording to Bruce and Trevor. That way they *have* to believe us."

"Great idea! Do you know anything about bugging?"

"Not really, but I'll bet it isn't hard to learn. I'm sure I can even order a bug over the Internet."

A few days later, I arrived early to work. Bun wasn't there yet. So far, so good. I planted the bug where I thought she wouldn't be able to detect it.

Next, I went to my office to call Reggie to find out what information he dug up about Eternal Treasures when I had called him before. The fact is with all the excitement, I had forgotten to get back to him after he left me a message. "Reggie. What the hell is going on with you? I haven't heard anything about the info I need. Am I taking away from your masturbation time?"

"Wha?" He yawned into the phone. "Hey, that's uncalled for. As a matter of fact Miss mean and nasty, I was going to call you today."

"Okay. I love you, too. What do you have for me?"

He yawned again. "To begin with, the business looks legit. But Bruce and Trevor have another company. They import diet supplements from Europe that aren't FDA approved in the U.S. They sell them over the Internet. My guess is this is a revenue stream for Eternal Treasures and the old junk they deal with there."

"They're artifacts, Reggie. You know, the old stuff like my mother's antiques, except much older."
"Like your mom?" He laughed at his own joke.

"No, never mind." *How in the world did he get to be so brilliant and still have no common sense?* "What about the symbols I sent you. Any luck there?"

"No way, I couldn't figure it out. I'm not even sure Einstein could translate them. Sorry, honey. No clue. I am calling in the heavy artillery."

"Thanks for trying. Let me know when the troops arrive."

The heavy artillery arrived in the form of the alphabet. Unbeknownst to us, H.T.H., as he is called, was fiddling around in the conflagration like Nero in Rome. He grew genuinely inquisitive and intense about every happening. We got a strange call from the hacker himself.

I imagined a very plump nerd with Mason jar glasses, eating M&M's with Mountain Dew. However, for all I know he could be a handsome dude no one would suspect.

"Egypt? This is H.T.H."

"Yes? What's going on?"

"Truthfully, I realized I'm interested in your company and its exploits. So I started digging deeper. Oh, call me Harry. A.K.A. Harry the Hacker."

"Well, come on, don't hold out. What did you find? Gina, it's H.T.H., Harry, himself," I mouthed.

"I looked up several of the people you mentioned. And I mean *really* looked up. Do you realize that not one of them shows up anywhere, again, no matter what?"

"That's not so unusual if they stay below the radar, is it?" I knew he would never uncover them. I dare not unleash the Kraken though.

"Come on, Egypt, they have to be somewhere. Even the census doesn't show any info on them," he blasted. "I'm glad I recovered that map for them because I found out Cryptonomics is into some shady businesses."

I blanched at his words, but knew his discovery had to be valid. I construed that from what I've heard.

"What? What is he telling you?" urged Gina as she watched my face go from interested to excitement.

106

"Wait, I'll put you on speaker phone. Gina, he says there's no info anywhere on our people. "*Of course, we were afraid of that,*" but Crypto is into some shady dealings. I think more dark than shady."

"Tell us more," she implored.

We were not going to be complacent though we had a rough going.

'The symbols in your records are ancient. That I know. Why they use them is another matter. I hope you aren't too angry, but I went ahead and emptied half of Crypto's funds into E.T's account to boost your company in whatever effort. I thought you'd appreciate it. That was a cinch."

"Oh, crap. Help us, Mary Magdalene. What if they suspect we did that?"

Gina whacked my side, "Egypt, E.T. knows we aren't knowledgeable enough to do that, I hope. And I'm not giving up my inheritance. Cripes, our gig is getting in trouble," she reminded me. "Are they going to suspect us, Harry?" she added anyway. We weren't going to be complaisant about it either.

With a swagger in his voice, H.T.H. replied, "Never happen, doll. All's well with the world. So go ahead and do your thing with E.T. They're far ahead of this crazy and secretive game of Crypt Keepers."

"Huh?" Both Gina and I shuddered.

"Hey, you paid me a heap, so your secret's safe with Harry. I may not know all, but enough to glean that info." It sounded as if he had a sense of confidence with a wide grin accompanying it. "I don't falter, I punish the wretched. I assure you."

"Okay, Harry, thanks. Double thanks. We'll wait until it all tumbles down. We'll send you a bonus for this above and beyond performance."

"Hey, no problem, ladies. Catch you on the flip side."

After I hung up, we looked at each other for what seemed like eons. Finally, Gina spoke. "Holy Ghost, shine on us now! What's going to happen?"

CHAPTER EIGHTEEN

The day arrived for us to move to Scranton. I hated giving up my beautiful apartment, even if it would be saved for us to use when we were in New York. It wouldn't be the same. New York? Scranton? No contest. Then there were the looming family issues to be dealt with and a few undesirable acquaintances. We vowed to steer clear of them as much as possible.

"Oh, Gina," I complained. This means I'll be forced to eat my mom's overcooked roast beef. It's so overdone, I'm sure she wants to make it so the steer never made noise again."

"Well," said Gina. "I've had your mom's desert roast beef. I agree, except that the gravy is even worse. Still, she makes a mean apple pie."

"Not enough to make me want to live there again."

***

After we arrived in Pennsylvania and unloaded our luggage, Gina and I rambled on to our new but temporary home.

"Well, here we are, Gina, right back in the same place we worked so hard to flee. Ain't this just great, or what?"

Gina put on a plastic smile, probably to hide how miserable she was feeling. "Bruce said it would be temporary. And, it isn't like we have to *live* at home.

We have a company condo, remember?"
"That's some consolation anyway."

We stopped in front of an almost new condo complex; slightly upscale.

I checked the address. The keys had been given to us before we left.

"Wow!" I exclaimed stepping inside. Fully furnished, open grate skylight, and a large kitchen. *If only I could cook anything other than tacos. Maybe I could hire a chef.* It had a formal dining room, family room, a good size master bathroom and the bedrooms were the best.

Gina stood wide-eyed, too. "I didn't know they had places like this here."

"What's this?" I picked up a note from the coffee table.

Egypt and Gina, we hope you enjoy your new home. We will see you on Monday at the new offices. We have another mission for you--Bruce and Trevor.

***

On Monday, Bruce called me into his office and relayed our assignment. I was both relieved and disappointed. No exotic location. Safer, but not as exciting. We were to go to an auction in Ohio and bid on a pair of Rookwood vases by Shirayamadani. I loved his work. His early vases were worth more than their weight in gold.

"You have your reservations." He handed me the envelope with instructions and hotel reservations. "Use your business credit card for any other expenses. It's a nice drive. I've reserved a car for you if you don't want to take Gina's." Bruce gave me the keys to a new Mercedes.

"Thanks. Is it okay for Gina to drive? She's keen on road trips. She loves to drive."

He grinned. "Sure, whatever you want."

"Just one more thing. What's my bidding limit at the auction?"

"Try not to bid over $8,000." He looked at his watch. "If that's all, I have a meeting in a few minutes."

"See you when we get back." I turned and left.

Gina was waiting in my office. "Hey. What's the assignment? Paris? Moscow? Tahiti?"

I laughed. "Not so romantic this time. We're going to drive to Ohio—an auction—to buy some vases."

"Huh?" Gina screwed up her face. "Vases? Ohio?" She dropped into a chair. "Ohio?"

"It's not so bad. It's safer and I think I need a break from the adventure for a little while."

Gina looked distracted. "Wait a minute. I remember that Craptonomics has its headquarters in Canton, Ohio. Hah! Coincidence? I think not."

I settled on the sofa. "I think Ohio is just where the vases are and it has nothing to do with Cryptonomics."

She looked at me and pursed her lips. "If you say so."

***

As we stood in line at the auction, waiting to receive our paddles, Gina elbowed me.

"Ow! What was that for?" I rubbed my arm.

"Shhh. Listen." Gina pointed to a tall man at the registration desk.

"What? I don't hear anything." I thought she was imagining things.

"He just registered as Julian Woods—from Cryptonomics." Gina whispered.

"Really? Well, this is a fortunate coincidence. Let's sit close to him and his 'friends.' Maybe we can collect some intel for Bruce and Trevor."

Gina gave me a thumbs up and winked.

After signing in and receiving our paddles, Gina and I managed to sit right behind them. Unfortunately, the little we heard was in another language. *Come on guys, how about a language I can understand fully. French? German? English would be great.*

They must have gotten my mind message because suddenly they switched to English. I listened carefully. I took out a note pad and wrote a message to Gina. *Looks like they want to stir things up with Eternal Treasures. They're after the same vases we are. I think they said something about them getting more money from a private source.*

Gina made a face and scribbled a reply. *What scumbags.*

An older man in an expensive grey suit came over and sat next to the tall Crypto man holding the paddle. "The money is power. It is imperative that we beat *'them'*. Failure is not an option."

He glanced around to make sure he wasn't overheard then continued. "They made it easy for us to keep collecting information from them. They are lacking brains and common sense." He gave a wheezy laugh.

"The man with the paddle answered in a low voice. "They're all over the place. It's hard to know what they're doing and how much money they've made. Our people come first. Winner takes everything. Triumvirates, first and foremost." He flung his hand in the air almost like a Nazi. They went on.

"By the way, Keenan, I got texted that there is extremely important business to look into. They said they could not tell me until we came back."

"Damn, it sounds like bad news. We're so close."

Who in the world are the Triumvirates?

My musing was interrupted when the Shiryamadami vases came up for bid. I raised my paddle for $1,000. The Crypto guy upped to $1500. The price kept rising. After $4,000 it was me and baldy. I bid $7,000. *Cripes, almost at my limit.* Two Crypto men turned and glared at me.
The bid rose to $8,000. I couldn't help myself. Maybe it was temporary insanity but I raised my paddle for $9,000. Crypto guy shook his head and gave up. It was ours.

I blew out a breath of relief that it was over.

Gina looked puzzled. "What did you do to get the vases? That guy talked so fast, I couldn't understand him."

"This is your first auction, isn't it?"

Gina tipped her chin upward. "Yes. So?"

"So, you get used to the talk and it makes sense after a while. And this auctioneer wasn't even that fast. You should hear some of them. The bidding process is—

"Wait! I see jewelry."

Her eyes lit and her ears perked up like a rabbit that heard a hawk. We had to stay for the jewelry auction. She bid on a pearl necklace and a 17th century set of blue topaz earrings.

113

My mind wandered. *Did I make a big mistake in bringing her? Now she'll want to go to every chic auction in the country. Geesh.*

When Gina had won several pieces she wanted, she turned to me with a grin. "I think that's enough. Looks like furniture coming out next. Ready to go?"
"I have been for the past hour. Oh crap, Gina. Bruce is going to kill me. I went $1,000 over his limit. But I couldn't let our competition take those vases. It would be like, like, I don't know, a mortal sin or something, right?"

Gina put on her wise face. "Considering the circumstances, I don't think so. It was only a thousand dollars. Not much from Eternal Treasure's budget, I'm guessing. Especially after what H.T.H. did."

"So then, I don't need that pair of rosaries my mom made?"

"Hell, no, she has a pipeline to the Pope for heaven's sake. We'll be fine."

Oddly, her words made me feel better. *I wonder if Crypto examined their bank account lately, I was jabbering in my head.*

CHAPTER NINETEEN

All the way home I worried about the thousand dollars over budget. The next morning I squared my shoulders and told him.

"Hey, don't look so scared." Bruce gave me a bright smile. "That's nothing. I'm glad you hung in there. $9,000 is a bargain for those vases." He stroked the crate that packed the vases as if it were gold.

I left Bruce's office and headed for mine. Just as I opened my door, my cell phone rang. Gina babbled hysterically.

"Flat tires, flat tires! All the air leaked out and not on its own," she squealed. And worse! There are political stickers all over them. I'm so pissed."

"Slow down, Gina. What happened?"

I heard her take a breath.

"I went to Mom's house to drop something off and left the car running. I was only there a few seconds. When I returned the tires were all flat and covered with ugly stickers. Ugh! They disgust me."

"Do you know who could have done this?"

"I'll bet it was Betty Jean Tanners, that bitch. How did she know I'd be there? I swear she's bugged my phone."

"What about the stickers?" I looked at the clock. I had work to do but Gina needed me so I settled in until she could calm down.

"They're all over the car. Ugly political stickers—and not even our party. It's the other one—the *wrong* one."

She sobbed. "Now I have to get the car over to detail and hope they can do something to fix this mess. I'll be into the office as soon as I can."

There was a silence.
"Gina?"

"Uh, yeah?"

She sounded calmer.

"You know. I was due for a new car anyway. This one was starting to bore me."

"So Betty Jean is forgiven?"

"Hell, no! I'm going to make her pay. It's the intention that's important here."

"Gina. This isn't high school anymore. Be the grown-up here and let it go."

"Well, since you put it that way. I guess I'll drop it. I know how she found me. She probably had Gregory follow me. She'll never forgive us for taking that picture of her hairy ass under the bleachers."
"Probably Gregory and the picture. I'll come and get you. Call the detailers and AAA right now. Don't worry. It'll work out fine. The best revenge for Betty Jean is to not let her see you upset. It's what she wants."

"Mm-hm. See you in a few."

I disconnected and looked at the clock again. *Should I tell Bruce? No. He won't miss me for a few minutes. Cripes. I never heard of anyone holding a grudge for as long as that mongo hairy-assed Betty Jean.*

I rushed to the car. When I gripped the steering wheel, something didn't feel right. "What the...." My hands were stuck to the steering wheel. Somehow Betty Jean had slipped past security, and put super-glue on the steering wheel. "How did she do this? Where was security? Damn. That's what I get for buying a convertible."

Thinking fast, I did the only thing that came to mind. I sat there beeping the horn with my nose while singing, "Burning Down the House."
It took only a minute for the security guard to come running. He called the paramedics. They extracted my hands with a foul smelling chemical and took me to the ER. My hands are red and raw. They slathered them with an antibiotic salve and bandaged me up. What else could go wrong today? Betty Jean needs to learn a lesson."

I went back to our apartment and called Gina and Bruce to explain what happened. Gina was livid and ready to kill Betty Jean.
"Do you need a ride home? I called Mom after AAA came and took the car to detailers. I explained over the phone what to do. They said it will be ready in the morning. We can pick you up."

"Thanks but I already called a taxi. I can't drive with my hands so sore. See you at home."

***

Trying to open my apartment door with bandaged hands was a challenge and I silently cursed myself for not taking Gina up on her offer of a ride. I finally managed the door. Gina wasn't home yet so I changed into a loose robe then relaxed in front of the television. *Oh Lord and Master, what can happen now?*

***

117

"Huh? Wha?" Gina was gently shaking my shoulder.

"Egypt. Wake up."

"Oh. Sorry. The doctor gave me some pain meds. They must have put me to sleep. What time is it?"

"Around eight. I brought us sandwiches from the deli."

"Thanks. I'm starving." I unwrapped a sandwich gingerly. My hands hurt and I was fuming mad at Betty Jean. "You know, vandalizing a car with stickers and flat tires is one thing. It doesn't cause bodily harm. This!" I held up one hand, "is another matter. I won't be able to work for days."

"I talked with Bruce," said Gina. "He said to take as much time as you need to heal."

***

A couple of days later, I was rewrapping my hands with new bandages. They were healing really well and I was sure I could go back to work soon. My cell phone rang.

"Egypt. Come down to the carport."

"Why?"

"Just come down, please?"

I finished my bandaging and hurried to the carport. There was Gina in a brand new Corvette convertible—midnight blue. And air brushed on it was a constellation. Neat.

"Wow! This is beautiful. What are you going to do with the Porsche?

Gina grinned from ear to ear. "To hell with the old Porsche. I'm selling it. This is soo much more elegant and racy."

"Good for you. Maybe Betty Jean will buy it. After all, it's her 'party' We both burst out laughing.

"Get in. Let's go for a ride."

I slid into the soft, leather seats. "This is amazing."
Gina peered at me. "What's the matter? I can tell when you're covering up a bad emotion. . . . You didn't go and see your mother, did you?"

I lowered my eyes.

"Egypt! You said you weren't going to see her unless it was with other family members present."

I shrugged. I know, but she sounded so lonely when she called. I caved. I'm so repentant."
"Well?"

"I think she's losing her mind. She swore she saw Jesus in her English muffin. When I couldn't see it, she went into a rage. She ensconced it in the freezer for posterity. The rosary flew out of her pocket and she started praying over it. Just like the time she saw the Blessed Mother in the soapy sink. And she kept that cinnamon bun in the freezer that looks like Jesus. They're everywhere. But dad keeps smiling about it. I'm worried about her mind."

"I'm sure it's nothing. She's always been a bit of a religious fanatic. Basically, she's a good person. Let it go and forget it. And, don't go over without other people there."

"You're so right." I leaned back in the seat and enjoyed the ride. When we returned home, I made a decision. "I'm going back to work tomorrow. I have use of one hand and the other is getting better really fast. I'm bored. I miss my work."

"I'll bet Trevor and Bruce will be glad to hear that."
"Trevor has called twice a day since this happened. He's been really great. I got flowers this morning. Yellow roses. Don't think I don't see the looks you and Joey give one another either. I know when something is cooking."

She smiled and gurgled, "Yea, it's great. He's a doll."

Gina gave me a knowing look again and turned onto a country road and she floored the gas pedal.

Scary, but loads of fun with our hair waving furiously in the air and yelling out, "Let 'er rip!" With anyone else I would have been terrified, but Gina handles a car like a NASCAR pro.

CHAPTER TWENTY

Gina wasn't in the office, so when Bruce handed me the next assignment I was thrilled to see that it would be in New York. I called her right away. "Hey best girlfriend. Guess what! Our next assignment is in New York City."

She squealed, "Really! That's the best. Can we drive there—in my new Corvette?"

"You bet."

"When is it?"

"We leave in two days and will be gone probably three."

"Great, I'll call my family and tell them. Goody, no dinner with them this Sunday."

"See you at home tonight." I disconnected then called my mother. Thankfully, she wasn't home. I left a message hoping that would be enough."

***

On the road, driving as fast as we could, when feasible; I had noticed more than one man ogling Gina's sexy car with sheer jealousy on their faces. When one dorky Neanderthal leered at us, I yelled over, "Suck our exhaust." Gina floored it and zipped past him.

I flung my arms up. "Freedom! We're riding off into the sunset, sunrise, and everywhere we can!"
I glanced at the speedometer as we zipped along a country road near a small town—90 MPH. "I know this is a blast, but maybe we should slow down a bit. Speeding tickets are

definitely not cool. We aren't on the salt flats. Mayberry cops can be ruthless."

"You got it." She let off the gas and turned up the Sirius Radio to blasting rock music.

Wrrrr, Wrrr, Wrrr.
I turned to see red flashing lights behind us. "Too little, too late."

"Damn." Gina slowed and pulled to the side of the road.

As the patrolman approached the car, Gina pulled off her sunglasses. I guessed it was because she wanted him to see her sorrowful, beautiful, and innocent-looking eyes. I relaxed. Gina was a master at getting out of tickets.

The patrolman stopped by the window. I couldn't see it but I knew her doe eyes were sparkling like chocolate diamonds.

"Driver's license and registration, please."

License and registration in hand, he stared at her a minute then walked around the car, studying it. When I looked into his eyes, I saw a familiar glazed look—one that Gina almost always seemed to bring out in men in a minute, whenever she wanted.

"Well, Miss. You were going ninety. Way faster than the speed limit in our little town. I know your car just cries out to go fast, but you really need to watch that lead foot."

Gina leaned closer to him. "Oh, officer. I'm really embarrassed. This is a new car and I'm not used to the way she handles. I didn't realize how fast I was going."

I was sure she was batting her long, thick eyelashes at him.

He colored bright red and smiled. "Hmmm. I see. Understandable, Miss Scarpetta." He handed her license and registration back. "I'll let you off with a warning this time. But keep a close watch on that speedometer." He tipped his cap then ambled to his patrol car and drove off.

"Well, strip my gears. The almighty Gina Scarpetta in action is a wondrous thing to behold."

Gina tipped her head down and gave a big *whoosh*. When she looked up there was a sinister smile plastered on her face. "High five, baby, I did it again. That was close. Another speeding ticket and I will lose my license."

She put the car into gear and drove off.

"You rock, my friend." A little way down the road, driving at a modest speed, we both broke down and guffawed. To be honest, being a blue-eyed long haired blonde made it easy for me to get away with a lot, too. Then we broke out singing.

***

At Eternal Treasures, Trevor and Bruce called Peter. He sat at his desk eyeing a small, electronic gadget. Say, Bruce. "Have any idea who could have planted a second bug on Myrtle's desk?"

"Ah," said Bruce. "I can give you one guess—our company's own two-lady spy team, E & G, Inc." He smirked and shook his head.

"I should have guessed. Well, maybe this is a good thing. It might give them more info on what's going on. Maybe that can be useful to us. Fresh ideas and such."

"Good thinking. Put it back where you found it and pull ours. We don't want them to know that we are on to them—not yet, anyway."

"Will do. I have enough on Myrtle to call immigration, but it would be better if we had more names and gleaned more info."

"I agree. We could hold a green card over her head after she talks like a politician without a microphone. She can work elsewhere. Want to be here when that happens?"

"You bet," said Peter. "Those women are something else. They're trying to take my job," he laughed.

"Great."

"Uh, when should we tell Egypt and Gina?"

"Not right now. I want to find out what they have up their sleeves. Us telling them to stay out of it is like telling a cat not to chase a mouse. We have to watch them carefully. Remember we promised to keep them safe—not an easy task with these two. If they get hurt, our heads will be on a platter, and not a silver one."

CHAPTER TWENTY-ONE

Our New York trip was turning out to be a blast and now we were ready to dig more into what Myrtle was up to. Early in the morning, I retrieved our bug from her desk. That night Gina and I listened to the latest recordings that had been transferred to a phone I bought just for this purpose.

"Wow! This is the most incriminating stuff, yet," said Gina.

"It sure is. I think it's time we had a talk with that Mata Hari."

We waited until she came in and settled into her chair before calling her into my office.

"What for?" she said with suspicion in her voice.

"Nothing, I am having a problem with a file on my computer. I thought you might know what something means."

She didn't look convinced, but came anyway.

After she sat down, Gina quietly locked the door.

"What is this all about?" She started to stand up but I stood in front of her.

"I think it's time we had a chat about what you've been up to."

We played the incriminating recordings of her conversations back to her.
She looked terrified. "What do you two girls have to do with any of this? It's none of your concern."

"How we are involved is not *your* concern. We have friends in areas of business that could think of more drastic ways to find out what we want to know."

She frowned. "No, no. I will tell you nothing. Do you realize what can happen to me if I breathe anything about our missions? They might already be planning to erase me for being stupid enough to be found out by amateurs." She crossed her arms over her chest. No. I will speak no longer. I will go back home to Albania."

"If we allow you," I told her.

She snapped her mouth shut tighter than an uncooked clam.

After fifteen minutes, we couldn't get anything more from her. Even threatening to go to Bruce and Trevor didn't open her up.

Not knowing what else to do, Gina unlocked the door. "So it's back to Albania for you, Miss Traitor. You think?"

I wasn't sure if she'd try to defend herself or run out on the company.

Myrtle hurried out nearly tripping over her own feet.

"At least I think we have her scared," I breathed. "We have to get to the bottom of this Russian drug mix-up now that Albania has been brought into the picture and blown their cover." At this point I was feeling like Sherlock Holmes, with Gina as Dr. Watson.

"We have to move carefully," I said as I paced my office. "The Russian mob is known for its cruelty."

Gina sat down. "This scares me."

"Aha!" I pointed a finger to the ceiling. "Perhaps we could convince Uncle Max or Uncle Quarto to help us. After all, well, he is in the import export business, right? *Sure he is I told myself*. I think we really need them. But will they say yes, or just lecture us to stay out of it? I don't know but we have to try."

"You have to be kidding, right?" asked Gina. "Uncle Quarto? The spy eye? The hawk who would keep us both home until we were forty? God forbid. The Holy Trinity has fewer eyes than him."

"True, we don't want to spend eternity in purgatory," I admitted. "Then everyone would find out. Damn."

"Well, keep it in mind if it comes to drastic measures." I sat behind my desk and whirled the chair around. "Okay, let's think about what we really have on Myrtle."

"Fine." Gina sat back and folded her hands in her lap.

"The best clue we have is her saying, 'We have to get more money to beat this company. Otherwise, there will be much damage. The payout for us is enormous. We can't lose that. Even now Eternal Treasures is approaching everyone with caution. They are continually changing their plans. We were told to throw them off their game. So far I don't think we have succeeded. There is a lot at stake for us.'

"We keep hearing: more money, money. And what damage? Who or what are they going to damage?" I threw up my hands. "Too much trauma drama. The Albanian problem isn't quite over, I'll bet. However, I don't think we'll have to worry as much about them now. Well, at least Bun Bitch is out."

Just when we were about to plan our next move, Bruce called us to his office. When we got there, he was sipping a coffee and looking over some papers.
"Gina, Egypt. You, Egypt, will most likely be jubilant with your next assignment. You leave for Cairo on Friday."

I could hardly contain myself. You mean Egypt, Africa, right? Not Egypt, Ohio or New York?"

He laughed. "Good one. Not Ohio. I need you to deliver some papyri to the museum in Cairo. Pretty sure it will be an easy job. No danger, adventure, or problems."

"Thanks!"

"Oh, by the way, Myrtle is no longer with us. We discovered that she didn't have a green card. And, I'm sure, since you bugged her desk, that you know she was up to no good. She has decided to return to Albania."

"How did you know?" I asked with my mouth agape.

"You can't keep secrets around here. We know more than you think. We have been investigating her lately. Peter found the bug you put under her desk." He leaned forward. Anything we should know about? But I told him that his job is safe," he chortled.

"Well, if you have had her under surveillance then you know about as much as we do."

"Probably so, but I'd like to hear your audio anyway."

"Sure thing, I'll send it right over to you."

"You know, Egypt, Gina, we are as anxious as you to put an end to the gang and somehow turn them toward Cryptonomics. Myrtle is one down and at least one to go. There are others working on that aspect."

As Gina and I walked back to our office we passed Trevor in the hallway. "Egypt, may I speak with you in private?"

"I'll just go ahead," said Gina. After she turned the corner, he led me into his office.

"Egypt. I can't get you out of my mind, no matter what I do. I know there are some things you don't understand—like me not asking you out again. Plus many other dealings I can't talk about right now. I'm begging you to ignore them."

"Well, I just decided that you weren't interested after all. I thought we had a connection, but"

He wrung his hands in frustration. "There *is* a connection. It's just complicated right now, that's all. When you get back from Cairo, can we meet somewhere out of town? Please. Give me another chance."

My heart melted. He reminded me of a puppy that had lost its toy and desperately wanted it back. I wasn't sure what "complications" he was speaking about but it is against the rules for employees to date. I bet he has caught Bruce doing the same at some point. That rule glared at me saying go ahead, do it, Egypt. Another dare to do it, unadvisable moment for me.

"Egypt?"

"Well, sure. When I get back we can go somewhere and really talk about this." I tried to sound disconnected and cool, but my heart was pounding at the thought of being with him.

CHAPTER TWENTY-TWO

On the day before Gina and I were to fly off to my favorite destination in the world—Egypt, I arrived at work bright and early. Passing Myrtle's empty desk gave me a warm glow inside. *Gina and I had a hand in that solution. Good riddance Bun Bitch.* When I opened my door and turned on my computer, there was an urgent message from Bruce. "See me in my office as soon as you get in. Bring Gina."

Huh? Gina wouldn't be in for another hour. I texted her. "Better come as soon as you can. I know you wanted to linger over another cappuccino this morning, but Bruce wants to see us, pronto."

A minute later, she replied. "On my way. What???"

I didn't answer. When she rushed in, looking like she just stepped out of *Elle* magazine, I wondered how she did it. It took me at least an hour to look even close to as elegant and polished as she did.

I didn't wait a second. I crooked my arm in hers and turned her around. We hurried to Bruce's office.

"Did we do something wrong?" Gina whispered.

"I don't know but it could be bad."

I knocked then opened the door. "Bruce?"

"Egypt. Gina! Have a seat. Would either of you care for a cappuccino?"

"You read my mind," said Gina.
She whispered, "*I didn't finish mine.*"

"Uh, sure. Thanks," I said with uncertainty. *What is this about?"*

He pressed a button on his console then settled into his chair. "How are you both? Up to any snooping I might be interested in?" He grinned.

A moment later, a young woman I hadn't seen there before brought in a tray of cappuccino and pastries.

"Will there be anything else, sir?" She looked at us questioningly.

"Nothing, Alice. Thank you." He gestured toward us. "This is Egypt and Gina, our head researchers."

Alice smiled and nodded. "Good to meet you. This is only my first day and already I've heard about what you did in Italy."

I wasn't sure whether that was a good thing or a bad thing. Were we going to be reprimanded for interfering with a mission? We couldn't have just left Luigi there to fend for himself.

Bruce handed us cups of steaming goodness and gestured for us to help ourselves to a pastry. I grabbed a delicate cinnamon square and a blue napkin.

"I suppose you wonder what this is about." Bruce had a cryptic look on his face. "I have discussed your service to Eternal Treasures with the other management members and we agree that you have gone above and beyond your agreed-upon service. Egypt, you have proven yourself to be courageous, brave, and willing to take extreme risks to do what you think is right."

"Okay, um, th-thanks." I stuttered with a mouthful of crumbs.

He turned to Gina. "And you, Gina have been right there with her all the time and willing to join in whenever you are needed."

Gina just smiled, leaned back in her chair and winked at me.

"Well, in light of what happened in Italy when you both saved the life of Luigi, I would like to offer you, Egypt, a raise in salary." He handed me a folded card. "Beginning immediately."

I unfolded the card and almost choked. My salary had nearly doubled. "Oh, my. Thank you!"

"Gina," he said, I would like to offer you a bonus." He handed her an identical folded card.

She opened it. The corners of her mouth turned up. "Thank you very much, but I don't deserve this, plus, since I'm a woman of independence, I would rather it go to Egypt. She did more than I did. She's always the one who rushes in to do the right thing."

I put my cup on the tray. "Gina, thank you, but you *do* deserve it." She gave me that stare—the one that says, "Don't argue. You can't win this one.'" So I backed down. "Thanks, Gina. Thanks, Bruce."
I thought that this might be a perfect time to bring up something else. "I have something I'd like to discuss." I cleared my throat and poured a small glass of water from a pitcher on the cart with the pastries and cappuccino. "I'd like Trevor to be here, too."

Gina turned to me and whispered, "Are you sure this is the right thing to do?"

I ignored her.

"Well, I'm not sure where this is going, but okay." He paged Trevor.

A minute later, Trevor strode in. When he saw me, he looked terrified. He pulled up a chair and sat down.

I brushed crumbs off of my skirt. "Well, as you have stated, Bruce, Gina and I have done a lot for the company and found ourselves in some dangerous situations on more than one occasion. What we know about the company is that you deal in returning antiquities—for which you receive handsome returns. You auction beautiful and valuable items and you have a hand in a small diet pill venture and a security company."

Bruce and Trevor stared at us so wide-eyed I thought their eyes might pop out, bounce onto the floor and roll out the door.

"We also know you are in competition with a company called *Cryptonomics.*" I snickered. "I call them the 'Crypts' because they are hooligans, like the street gang. In the process you are trying to amass a lot of money for a reason we aren't clear on—something about a tomb and a device. But, your passion for this project trumps anything else."

Bruce leaned forward. "Egypt—"

"Please let me finish." He nodded and gestured for me to continue.

"You gentlemen are hiding something. Don't you think it's time to trust us enough to let us in on what that is?" I gauged their expressions. *Not angry or suspicious. That's a good sign.* "You know we'll just keep digging until we find out. Wouldn't it be easier and safer to just let us in on the secret?"

Bruce and Trevor looked at each other, eyebrows raised, as if some sort of silent communication passed between them.

"Wow!" said Bruce. "I'll be damned." He stood and rounded his desk to be directly in front of us. He poured himself another cappuccino. "Egypt, Gina. We know you deserve answers, but those to whom we must answer to have given us strict orders to *not* reveal certain things because they could put you in danger. Please trust us just a little longer. I'll arrange a meeting for when you get back from Cairo to discuss this more."

Trevor nodded to Bruce then turned to us. "You are right in your assessment of what we are about. We have a map we're following and Cryptonomics, with the help of a mole we caught, stole a part of it. We have to pretend that we don't have it, but we actually wanted them to steal it to throw them off their plan. We are trying to preserve a potential harmful *(boy, do I mean harmful)* event. We wish them to change the direction they were headed, which unfortunately was near the correct one. I know it's confusing, but wait until you get back, please."

Bruce added to what Trevor said, "Cryptonomics is a company that is fueled by greed and will stop at nothing to get what they want—even murder. I promise you, there will be answers when you get back."

I let out a long breath. "Gina?"

"I think that's fair."

Trevor looked especially relieved. "Thanks."

I stood. "Well, I guess we'd better get back to work. There's a lot to do before we leave for Cairo."

"We'll see you when we return," said Gina.

We left the office and closed the door behind us. I was shaking like a leaf. "It was hard to keep my cool, but you! You just sat there like a goddess. I so want your bravery."

"What are you talking about, girl. You're the bravest woman I've ever known. I was actually terrified. I kept it all inside though."

CHAPTER TWENTY-THREE

After a long plane trip and massive jet lag, I was ready to put my feet to sand. We were checked into a palace of a hotel—the venerable Mena House. We could see the Pyramids from our window. Stately and grand, I felt like we were in a classic movie.

After cleaning up and resting for an hour, I wanted to explore. I called down for a taxi to take us around. The hotel said that Eternal Treasures had provided a driver and a car. I was hoping it would be air-conditioned.

Over the next few days, before my appointment at the museum we visited the Valley of the Kings and Queens. We trekked to the ancient sites like thirsty dogs lapping up water. I felt as if I was wrapped in a dream—a hot, dusty dream—but one I would treasure the rest of my life. I didn't want to think about having to leave.

At the pyramids, I was breathless. I envisioned ancient Egyptians laboring to pull the sleds that carried huge stone blocks. I saw their muscles ripple under sweat-glistened skin as they pulled in unison. The experience of standing in the shadow of the great pyramid was exhilarating beyond any expectations. Then there is the great Sphinx. I stood a long time drinking everything in. But, I thought, maybe an anti-gravity device did this. You know aliens and all. No one will ever be certain about how these miracles were accomplished.

Gina enjoyed it, too. Shopping in Cairo was a dream come true for her. Designer wear, exotic perfumes, beautiful leather goods—all for a fraction of the cost in the States. To her credit, she never complained about the heat, the dust, the smells, or the lack of modern conveniences in some sectors. She had learned and endured a lot. Those archaeology magazines I had strewn all over our apartment on purpose had been a fantastic learning tool. She had done it on her own.

On the day of my appointment at the Cairo Museum, I dressed modestly in khaki slacks, white shirt, and sandals. I carried my package with care. The meeting went well and we were given a tour of the museum by the director. I was taken into the back to view the mummies not on display. "Wow" was all I could say.

The exhibit of King Tut's tomb findings was incredible. No photographs could do it justice. The sheer amount of gold in the mask, the tomb, the chariot, and in the funerary objects boggled my mind. I had visited the actual tomb. He was a warrior. They had his chariot and many bows and arrows. It seemed impossible that all that fit into the tiny space they had come from.

The mummy of King Ramesses was spectacular. It was so well preserved I felt as if I had been transported in time.

Before we left, I wrote a letter to Dr. Hawassi, a former Antiquities Minister. He told me he might be at the museum when I was there. Luck was on my side. He was there. I summoned my courage and introduced myself.

"Dr. Hawassi?"

He turned and raised an eyebrow.

I told him how much I admired his work and about the papyri I had delivered.

He remembered my letter and thanked us for our service. I was a little disappointed when he looked at his watch and told us he was late for a meeting and must leave.

That night, I watched the pyramids from the balcony of my room. They painted a surreal picture in the sunset. They were mind-boggling. The scope of their dimensions and age were too much to wrap my head around. They are spectacular at sunset.

The next day we explored the temple at Luxor. It was beyond belief.

"Egypt?" said Gina. "You're going to break your neck if you keep straining to see the top of the obelisk." I nearly fell over laughing.

I was trying to read as many glyphs as far up as I could.

My hands touched the hieroglyphs on the columns and walls. "God, Gina. These were carved by someone thousands of years ago. Can you imagine?"

Gina ran a finger over one of the carved pillars. "Really? They look so new. They don't look aged at all." She peered close to them.

Some of the paint that originally made the temple a glorious rainbow of color was still clinging to a few places. I held my breath and imagined being there ages ago when the temple was new. TV programs have shown marvelous recreations.

After a rest and a refreshing meal, we were off to the KV63 excavation.

"We're going to look at people digging?" asked Gina, disappointed at the lack of shopping opportunities. She already had to ship a boatload of things home because of the sheer quantity. A plane would have been overloaded.

"It's not just people digging. This excavation is turning out to be a very interesting site. It was a storage chamber for mummifiers. They even found some clay seal impressions with part of the name of King Tut's wife, Ankhesenamuramun."

"That's interesting. I remember seeing her painted likeness on the golden chair in the exhibit at the museum. I love the fashions and the hair and jewelry. I bought some replicas."

I smirked. "I'm surprised you didn't clean out the gift shop."

She laughed.

"Did you know that only about one half of one percent of Egypt's treasures has been found? There are whole cities buried under the sand."

"That'll take a while to uncover," said Gina.

"Could be centuries. The more they dig, the harder it gets. Politics create a big challenge."

***

"Ah, come on, Gina. This is our only chance to ride a camel—in *Egypt*—the once greatest civilization on the planet."

She wrinkled her nose. "I...I don't think I want to do this."

"Please," I pleaded.

Reluctantly, she gave in. "Okay. Just for you, though. They smell and look like they're full of fleas."

"I think they're cute," I said in defense. "Besides, you probably smell weird to them."

She gave me a look of sheer disgust.

"You owe me, big time."

Our guide helped us up onto the kneeling camel. To me, the ride was smooth sailing. Gina complained every step about the bumpy ride and the smell.

I laughed so hard I cried when we came to the end of our trek. The gravity of the stop when the camel kneeled down with its front legs threw both of us forward. Gina, who refused to touch the animal, went flying over its head.

"It's not funny!" shouted Gina sprawled on the sand.

The guide rushed over to her. Only her dignity was bruised, the rest, aside from a little sand, she was unharmed. That didn't stop her from complaining a bit.
"Humph! There go my new khakis." She brushed at her pants. "Well, I guess they can be cleaned." She looked at me and laughed. "Never again, though, will I do something like this just because you begged."

"I'm glad I have photos before you went head over heels. I'll download them to Facebook tonight." I took a look at what I took shots of. "See." I held up the view for her to see. "You look downright regal."

"She peered at the preview "I do, don't I. Me. Queen of the desert."

I think you'll like the next thing. It's a ride down the Nile on a real barge. You'll feel like Cleopatra herself."

Gina brightened up. "Now, that sounds fine. Certainly better than those camels! Do we have time to go back to the hotel and rest a bit? I'd also like to clean up."

"Sure. We've got a couple of hours. After the barge, we'll fly to Abu Simbel."

"Abbie, who?" asked Gina.

"It's a magnificent temple that used to be on the Nile until the dam was built. To keep it from being destroyed, it was painstakingly moved inland to save it."

"Oh." Gina's eyes glazed over. "No chance of me sitting this one out, is there?"

"No chance. I'm not letting you back out only to complain later that you didn't get to see everything."
At the hotel, after Gina showered, she sat on a chair, madly texting.

"Who are you texting?"

"Me?" she blushed. "Okay. It's Joey."

"Joey? The bean counter?"

"Yeah. I miss him."

"Hey," I put my fists on my hips. "You've been holding out on me. It's even more than I realized."

"Well. I was going to tell you pretty soon. I didn't want to jinx it. He's a little slow to pick up on how I adore him. He only asked me out a few weeks ago."

"So this was the surprise you told me about?"

"Uh-huh. Sorry I didn't tell you sooner." She put her phone down.
"Forgiven. Especially since I have a secret, too."

"Oh, give, girl. What is it?" She slathered her hands with lotion.

"It's about Trevor and me. In spite of everything, we're going to meet when I get back—somewhere out of town. He wants us to give 'us' another shot. He said he couldn't stop thinking of me. That's good news because I have a hard time keeping him out of my mind."

"Holy hell. You go, girl. Don't pay any attention to what Bruce or the company says. Love comes first!"

"I have a good theory about some of what's been going on."

I poured a glass of bottled water and sipped the refreshing coldness. "I believe raising all this money has something to do with an archaeological expedition somewhere. Hmmm, sand, could it be..."

"Go on."

"Well, for one thing," I said, "Eternal Treasures hired me, someone who knows a bit about the subject. Then there's another company that's trying to beat them to it and need information from our company to find it. They hire mobs to trip us up. And, let's not forget all the safeguards. Although some of them haven't turned out to be so safe."

Gina put a finger to her lips for a moment. "Hmm. Sounds pretty good to me. So, all the other things happening are just on the periphery, don't you think?"

"Sure sounds like it. But we can't be sure at this point." I stopped and stared at her. "Since when do you use words like 'periphery'? Have you been reading those magazines I strewed around the apartment?"

"Thank you, I think. You're such a grammar freak." Gina pouted.

CHAPTER TWENTY-FOUR

Eternal Treasures Headquarters

Bruce was agitated. This meeting wasn't going the way he wanted it to. "Please! Can we stay on track?" he shouted over the noise of everyone talking at once.

The room grew quiet. "Thank you. Now, number one, we eliminated the Albanian problem. I wouldn't be able to say that without the help of some strong women we all know."

He turned to a young man who looked like he was hoping to disappear into the walls. "What the hell's going on with the Russian problem?"

Mickey cleared his throat and took a sip of water. Sweat beaded on his forehead. "You know how busy we've been. Our last try at getting in touch with one of the decision makers was fruitless." He rubbed his palms hard. "If we don't make a connection soon, there'll be more trouble than we can handle." He threw up his hands. "Sorry. I don't know what else to do."

Bruce saw how frustrated Mickey was and decided not to press further right now. "Well, just keep at it. You know we can't call in strangers."

He turned to a tall man with thinning blond hair that found the lady's desk bug. "Peter. What are you doing for the Russian situation? You're one of my best analysts." He glanced around the room. "You're all top computer geeks. Come on. There must be some progress."

Peter took in a long breath. "We're doing what we can. There's so much data to analyze. We need more help."

Bruce considered this a moment. "Okay. Hire and train more people if need be. Vet them well and give only the necessary information. This is a sensitive operation."

"You got it," said Peter with a grin.
Trevor spoke up. "We have to get to the bottom of this. You know how Magna Z gets when all the pieces are not in order. None of us want to be on her 'List,' now do we?"

Trevor poured himself water and scanned the room. "Personally, I wish Damon Breeze had this assignment instead of Magna. Damon, I can work with, but Magna insists on complete autonomy. She's not an easy woman to negotiate with."

"I agree," added Bruce. "Still, she's in pretty deep with Stash, who isn't pleased at some of her decisions."

Max stood. "If you need my division's help, we're here for you." *Stash?*
"I appreciate that, Max," said Trevor. "But you seem to have your hands full."

"Okay," said Max. "The offer is there if you change your mind." He sat down again.

"Keep in mind that Egypt and Gina are our most valuable assets. I'm sure they're sticking their noses in where they don't belong. Little do they know that we are counting on them."

A murmur spread through the room.

"Okay," Bruce clapped his hands together. "I want reports on my desk showing progress ASAP. Thanks for coming."

Trevor took Bruce aside. "Look at their faces, Bruce. There's a cloud hanging over the room like yesterday's cigar smoke. These men don't like being one-upped by women. These aren't your most enlightened men when it comes to gender equality."

"I know. But I'm getting pretty tired of this group's lack of progress.... Except for Max—there's none better. And, for sure let's not get Grandpa Stash on our backs! Maybe I put the fear into them today."

"I think mentioning Egypt and Gina as valuable assets did that," said Trevor with a sarcastic smile.

"Okay. Enough." Bruce went around to his desk and eased into the big, leather chair.

"On another topic," said Trevor. Anything new about the Hall of Records that Herodotus wrote about? It's a particular interest of mine. As long as we're going to be in Egypt we—"

"I don't think anyone knows. It may be a lost cause. Not likely to make a difference in our project anyway, so let's follow the plan—*the* map. It's possible we might uncover the Hall someday—if it really exists. So far, though, there's no real evidence. How about concentrating on our current objective? I promise we'll address the Hall later."

"Okay," said Trevor, pulling up a chair. "We have to be the first to arrive at these sites to make everything believable." He rubbed his chin and glanced at the ceiling. "I keep wondering, though, how our people could have been so careless as to leave such an important and potentially dangerous object with Cleo."

Bruce tapped a pen on his desk. "It's a mystery that probably won't be solved. The Triumvirates just don't care. They want it for themselves and they'll push their plans into action. The thought of hordes of them racing in makes me ill. Relocating Cleo should have been an easy job. But, like you said, we've got to just keep going and throw them off their game."

"Well," said Trevor, "we've been successful at that at least. They are completely thrown off track. Plus, they are trying to get to the site first—the wrong site."

CHAPTER TWENTY-FIVE

Gina and I returned to the states with regret that our stay couldn't have been longer. It seemed that there was so much more to explore. But, it was time to dig further with our sleuthing even if it was in Scranton for a short time. We sat in my office, waiting for Bruce to call us to the meeting.

"Gina. I'm going to call Reggie. It's time to bring in the alphabet again. I know we'll have to pay him—a lot more—but it's worth it."

"You mean Harry?" asked Gina. "No, it's no use. Remember, he told us all he could find. Even he isn't a miracle worker."

"Oh, damn, you're right. Harry has done maximum effort. And, oh, that money he transferred. It most likely put us ahead of the 'Crypts'. Now we need to hear what Bruce and Trevor have to say to us. Remember? We demanded answers."

"And if they don't?" Gina bit her lip.

"Well, we'll just have to threaten to leave the company. We're valuable to them. They won't let us go. But I don't think it will come to that."

"I hope not. I like working here. Say. Maybe, if we need to, we can get Cousin Guido involved." Gina chuckled and tugged at her sleeve.

There is a cousin Guido. Not funny. My intercom chimed. It was Bruce. "Egypt. Gina. Would you please come to my office?"

As we entered, Bruce waved us over to the couches. Trevor sat quietly, his left ankle resting on his right knee. He looked worried and was fidgeting a bit. Ricky and Joey were also there. Bruce paced back and forth. He looked scared.

After we sat down, Bruce fell into the red, wing-backed chair. He looked at us. "I remember the promise we made to you and we intend to keep it." He turned to Trevor and nodded.

Trevor sat forward. "It's been wonderful having you both work for us. You've gone above and beyond your job descriptions by putting yourselves out there time and time again to...he made finger quotes in the air...'save the day.' Because of this, coupled with your integrity and your convictions, we feel you have a right to know what's really going on."

"We're listening," said Gina

Trevor continued. "Some time ago, we came upon a rare map indicating the location to Cleopatra's tomb. Our source insisted on anonymity. The map, however, turned out to be wrong. This worked in our favor because we convinced Cryptonomics that the map was accurate. They are following this map. We have since uncovered the accurate one. We discovered the correct translation key. If Cryptonomics ever discovers that we are misleading them, we are all in danger."

I gasped and clasped my hand over my mouth. *The file I uncovered on my computer?*

Bruce added. "We were allowed to examine it for a short time then transferred it to our files. We did this in segments so Cryptonomics would think we were safeguarding the map. Fortunately, they took the bait."

"I don't understand," said Gina.

"We'll talk later," I whispered.

"We discovered that one of the pieces had gone missing from our system," said Bruce.

Trevor added. "We manipulated the culprits and convinced them through inter-office emails, that we were distraught and that they have the authentic map to Cleopatra's tomb."

"Wow." I was nearly speechless.

"Uh, there's more," said Bruce, who still seemed nervous. "Trevor. You tell them."
"All right. We are raising millions of dollars to fund our project in Egypt. This isn't an easy thing to do on the sly. We don't want Cryptonomics to find out that we are amassing enormous funds." With his statement he peered over to Bruce. I knew it had to involve the transferred money. "We have what I'd say are unique sources. Our connections in Egypt allowed us to procure the permits to dig and keep our names off the record."

"Now, we have to put on a show of trying to retrieve the piece that Crypto," Bruce grinned at me, "stole." They will be laughing at us; however, we will get the last one."

Trevor continued. "It's not just Cleopatra's tomb that we are interested in. There is something even greater there."

"What are you talking about?" squealed Gina.

I shushed her. "This is incredible!" I said to Trevor.

"They cannot be allowed to find the real tomb. There is something there that could be incredibly wonderful but dangerous if it falls into the wrong hands."

Something occurred to me that I didn't like. "Do you mean to say that we've been chasing rainbows?"

"No," said Trevor, "you have been a valuable part of this project. It is all worth the time and dedication you have put into it—unknowingly."

"I would just like to know how you came about the documents that pinpoint where Cleopatra's tomb is. And exactly why was she moved and by whom? Experts have been searching for centuries."

Trevor looked contrite and guilty. "I wish we could reveal our source but they insist on absolute secrecy. Bruce and I are the only ones who know. As for moving her, well, that's a puzzle we don't have the pieces to. Our only objective is to allow them to believe they are digging in the correct area and that we are not. As long as they keep busy we'll all be safe and perhaps our people will retrieve the object in the future. They will have literally tons of work hauling unforgiving and unyielding sand. Like a honey badger they'll chew off their tail to get what they want. The labor is futile."

"In the meantime," said Bruce, "we have had other problems—and not just with Crypto. You've helped with that and thanks to you our Albanian problem is completely resolved."

"Not a problem," I said in a daze. My mind was fixated on the possibility of finding Cleopatra's tomb.

Trevor leaned forward. "But, now we have to deal with the Russians before this whole thing blows up in our faces. They gave us one week to come up with their drugs. We know it's a hoax perpetrated by Crypto to slow us down but we can't take any chance of our plan being revealed. So, we are exploring all avenues. We're also behind schedule and that presents its own set of problems. One of the reasons we have kept you in the dark is for your own safety. I know you want more, but right now that's all we can say without putting all of us in jeopardy."

"Thanks, Trevor," said Bruce. "So, Egypt and Gina, does that clear up at least some things for you?"

"I'm not sure what to say. It does clear up a lot. Cleopatra is important. In fact, this discovery could be of unsurpassed importance. I'm sure I can speak for Gina, too, when I say that we're proud to be a part of this."

"Yeah," said Gina. "Even though it is a bit nef, nefari—"

"Nefarious?" I added.

"Right. We wouldn't want to be left out of this amazing discovery if it does happen."

I wondered if Gina really meant that or she just didn't want to let on that she was totally lost."

"I just have one more point of confusion," I said. "Why does this matter so much?"

"Okay. I can't say much but it has to do with something that is capable of incredible destruction. I mean *big* destructive forces."

I shrugged. "I believe you. If you promise to keep us in the loop without putting the project or any of us, including you, in danger when advisable." *Oh, I didn't say advisable. Yes, I did.* We're in one hundred percent."

"That's a relief," said Trevor."

"Is that it, then?" I asked.

Bruce looked at Trevor who shrugged and said, "This is as good a time as any."

"There's one more thing," said Bruce. "Remember I said that this new location was only temporary?" I nodded.

"It has become necessary to move us all back to New York. I hope you don't mind being taken away from your families so soon."

I couldn't help grinning. *Is he kidding?* "We go where the company goes, boss."

Gina and I left and went back to my office.

"Make sure the door is closed all the way," I said.

She gave it a little push. "Closed."

Then we high-fived it.

"Do you think we're being told the whole story?"

"Of course not. I saw the furtive glances between Bruce and Trevor. We'll just have to keep digging on our own." *This is more complicated than I thought.*

I was just about to brainstorm with Gina when Bruce called us back to his office. When we entered, he and Trevor were whispering to each other. They had a solemn expression on their faces.

Bruce looked up when he saw us. "Thanks for coming back. We've been discussing it and agree that we were wrong. You shouldn't be kept in the dark on the most important factor any longer." He gestured for us to sit. "You deserve much more."

"Okay. So spill," I said.

Bruce pulled up a chair. "You might not believe all we have to tell you—"
"And why wouldn't we believe you?" asked Gina. "We know you fudged a bit in the earlier meeting."

152

"Fair enough," said Bruce. "What we have to say will be a lot to absorb."

"So?" I asked. "Tell us."

Trevor started. "Egypt. I know you watch a lot of educational programs because of your love for ancient civilizations. I also know you watch science programs, too."

"And? Why is this relevant?"

"You told me your favorite scientist was Dr. Michio Kaku, right?"

"Yes, I remember that." I was becoming impatient.

"You might have seen something about an unusual theory that has been extremely controversial. We know this theory is correct."

"I still don't see what this has to do with anything." I sighed.

"Come on guys," said Gina "give it to us straight."

"Okay," said Trevor. "Every universe—"

"What do you mean 'every universe'" piped Gina. "There's only one. God said so or did so." She wrinkled her flawless brow. "Didn't he?" She turned to me for validation.

"Maybe not, Gina."
Trevor took charge of the conversation again. "Oh. There are many universes. No one knows how many. You see, they are enclosed bubble-like places invisible to all, but they are right there before you. The theory is that many of them have combined like a chain. Earth happens to be right within our grasp."

"What do you mean 'within our grasp?' asked Gina, who looked both confused and intimidated.

"By 'us' I mean the human race. The fact is that our ancestors, centuries ago, came from some other plane in the universe, liked this one, and stayed.

Others scattered the world but remembered their origins. Some became traitors to our principles of life. Our true people are extremely advanced in technology—far beyond what we can do today.

"A device we nicknamed the 'bubble-ripper' tore open a very small hole in our bubble. That led us into your world. Our ancestors were explorers and helpers. Most of our methods of accomplishing feats are lost to this world but we helped many ancients to achieve masterpieces in art and creative invention." He took a breath and stared at us as if to gauge our reaction.

"Go on," I said.

"Okay. We can't come out of hiding to help any longer. We would be captured and researched like lab rats for the technology we have knowledge of. We cannot give it to Earth. It is too dangerous. You would destroy yourselves. Recovering this device at Cleopatra's tomb is vital to the safety of everyone on the planet."

I was stunned. "Trevor. This is crazy. I mean, you're no different from us."

"You're right. Physically, we are the same."

"Pssst". It was Gina. She whispered in my ear. "Remember Harry couldn't find *these guys*? Maybe they're telling the truth."

154

That's impossible, isn't it? I mean, this sounds like a bad movie." But when I looked in Trevor's eyes, I knew he was telling the truth—no matter how crazy and fantastic it sounded. "Heavenly Mother Hathor. It is true." My mouth hung open like a beached fish.

"So," said Gina, "Who are you guys if you're not Bruce and Trevor?"

"We *are* Bruce and Trevor. There's just more to us than you thought. There are lots of 'our' people everywhere."

I started to feel dizzy. This was too much to take in. I held Gina's hand. She was trembling.

Bruce spoke up. "One of 'our' leading scientists is still working on the Ripper to probe a much larger opening to allow great numbers of people into *our* sanctum. We have no idea why he is doing this but we assume he has turned traitor. They are striving to procure the old one to further the project, which we heard is at a standstill."
He stopped and studied our faces. When we didn't react, he continued the story. "When Cleopatra died, it was us who took her body and buried her. We knew tomb robbers would try to take her body if we didn't, among other factors. She was important. But the weapon was left or dropped with her, and it was not tested as far as we know. Now 'everyone' seems to know this."

Trevor took up where Bruce left off. "Some traitors caught wind of this not long ago. We believe they found some of our ancestors' secret codes. They started searching for it. The leaders—the Triumvirates, have already taken over a part of our world and want to do the same to Earth. They must be stopped or they will allow hordes of their followers in. But that's not the worst. The device is untested and we all could be destroyed. So that's the reason for our ploy. Because they were getting too close to the target area, we resorted to this subterfuge about the burial chamber and its whereabouts."

"Why can't they build their own weapon?" I asked.

"Fortunately, the inventor left no trace of his plans or any instructions on how to build it. The traitors are trying. That's why they want it. No one has been able to duplicate it. If they had, we wouldn't be talking now."

"And where do you live? I mean your home, universe, planet or?" asked Gina.

"It's too hard to explain if you don't know the science behind the theory. It's really far away, yet close."
That seemed to satisfy Gina, somewhat, as she wasn't understanding much anyway.

"Well," I said. "Gina and I have a lot to talk about. I think we'll leave you two, now."

I had a hard time getting to my feet. I guess I was in some kind of shock. Gina looked unsteady, too. Both of us felt confused. We still loved our men and nothing would change that.

Gina and I went home, poured some really good wine and settled onto the sofa. We began discussing the fantastical story we were just told.

"We have to believe them, right?" I asked. "We have to keep helping them."

"I don't know. It sounds so crazy. Come on, another universe. I fathom that... it's…it's too science fiction. This is all so confusing. But I trust you. So I'll go along with whatever you decide."

She hugged me.

"Okay, then we forge ahead. I just hope you're putting your trust in the right people."

"Our trust, Gina. Ours."

CHAPTER TWENTY-SIX

Trevor made the excuse to Bruce that we had some business to discuss and we headed down the street a few blocks from the office to grab a quick lunch and talk about what he had planned for 'us.' Multiple universes didn't figure into this conversation.

"Egypt, I hope you'll be pleased. I found a wonderful restaurant and Inn in the Pocono Mountains. Is Friday evening a good time for you?"

I grinned. "Hmm. Well, let me see. I'll just check my appointment book." I scrolled the calendar on my phone. "Well, you're in luck. It looks like that night is free, Mr. Storm."

We both laughed.

"Gina and I have come to terms with the revelation and we are fine with what you told us. We accept you both for what and who you are. We admire your courage and determination and will help in any way possible."

"You don't know how glad I am to hear that. I was worried sick."

"Now I know why the company is called Eternal Treasures, because you are one."

He blushed and gave me a charming smile.

"Plus," I added, "Eternal Treasure's initials are E.T. How appropriate is that?"

***

The drive out to the inn was refreshing. We didn't say much but feelings were high. Love was raining all over us. It had a distinct feel of serenity and acceptance.

We enjoyed an incredible meal. The quaint inn was cozy with its warm colors and antiques.

Out of the blue, Trevor said, "I hope I'm not being too forward, but I booked a room for us."

"I'd be disappointed if you hadn't," I said.

At dinner, people paid little attention to us. It was like we blended in with the wallpaper. I was glad and relieved. As I ate, the prospect of being with Trevor afterward started jangling my nerves. *What if I'm not good enough? Is sex the same for his race of people?* All sorts of odd thoughts ran through my mind.

When dessert came, I savored it. "You know how much I like chocolate and this is my favorite. It's divine," I said in what I hoped was a low, sexy tone. Our meal was so cliché you'd think we were in a scene from the classic movie, Casablanca.

When he said, "You do look like you're enjoying every mouthful, my dear," I burst out laughing. Unfortunately, I spattered chocolate mousse all over his shirt.

Trevor laughed and wiped off his shirt. "It's a good thing I brought a spare."
He signed the bill with our room number and took my hand. We strolled outside in the garden. Walking arm-in-arm, we were silent for a while. After admiring the fountain, he turned to me. "Shall we go to our room?"

I didn't have to think about it. "Yes, I'm ready. There's a chill out here and I could use some warming up." I winked.

"If you're worried about what Bruce will say, don't. He has his own worries. It will be fine."

We strolled to our room, my head on his shoulder. After unlocking the old-fashioned door, we stepped inside. A four-poster bed with a canopy filled much of the floor space. The colors in the room were light aqua and copper with tiny hints of blue, green, and red. It reminded me of Egypt. *Did he plan this color scheme?*

The bed looked luxurious and inviting. Trevor had arranged for flowers to be strewn about the room. I was in love.
He gently placed my head on his shoulder and caressed my hair. He sighed. "Ah Egypt, you are the tastiest of forbidden fruit."

He removed my clothing, piece by piece with delicacy and respect.

As I worked on his shirt buttons, he whisked me up and carried me to the bed. He undressed and dove in the feather mattress with me.
Our first act was playful. We bounced around the softness of the deep mattress and laughed like schoolchildren.

After a while, we grew quiet and serious. Trevor took my face in his hands and kissed me deeply. "I love your eyes. Your curves and your forever legs make me want to beg for you. You are a beautiful and naughty girl. I am your lap dog."

He caressed my body, sending ripples of ecstasy through me.

I ran my hands over his lean body and lowered myself onto his chest. "Watch out. Your naughty master calls." I gave him a fiendish smile.

He gently slid his hands over my back and down while I combed my fingers through his hair and outlined his face with my tongue.

His fingers played me like a fine-tuned instrument. When he entered me I was filled with euphoria. We savored each other for a long time before we spent ourselves.

Afterward, we held each other tightly. Trevor stroked my hair and kissed my forehead without saying a word.

I hugged him, not wanting to let go. I had an unexplained feeling of foreboding afterwards. I felt as if I had captured a cup of sunshine, bright and beautiful that glowed on me. It was like a warm halo that enveloped my body, but the light might be turned off.

Trevor looked deep into my eyes.

"Trevor. What will become of us? How can we hide our feelings after this? I'm sure our eyes will give us away. What if something comes crashing down and destroys us?"

He kissed me. "We keep our minds on our goal. It will be fine. I promise."

***

The next morning I awoke and looked out the window. A mist hung on the landscape but it didn't erase the happy look on my face. That would have to be hidden as soon as we left here and went back to town. The tightness in my stomach screamed to recapture the previous night.

"Good morning," he said and pulled me close to him. "Remember. I will always love you no matter what."

I felt as if he saw right into my heart.

I whispered, "Me too."

CHAPTER- TWENTY- SEVEN

"Forgive me for I know not what I do dear Lord," I said as I looked up with my hands clasped in prayer. The only thing lacking was my rosary.

Gina, puzzled as hell, gave me a strange look, "What are you talking about?"

"Do you want these incompetents trying to figure what to do with the Russian mob, or should we execute our own plan?"

"Ahh, we have been successful before. They haven't found anything out or made headway. We heard they have only a short time to do it. They are afraid to be found out for who they are. I don't want anyone killed. So, if you're game...," Gina said as she stood stalwart.

We had a long discussion on what we would do.

When I first accepted the job, I never dreamed I'd be walking around warehouses looking for the one that belonged to a sinister force, but here we were. Naturally, "Girlfriend" volunteered to distract the watchman while I scoped out the location of both facilities. Never be certain you won't also need something like boots or sexy clothing on shrewd excursions. There would be plenty of other distractions too.

***

There we were, staking out the warehouse district in our fancy, unbuttoned, showing off our bodies, trench coats. We figured this undercover or not so undercover method wouldn't give us away as dumb chicks unless we angled that role, which can come in handy in perilous situations. I found in a roundabout way from Trevor the location of our warehouse. The key was altogether another ball of hard wax.

"Did you know no one has been to ours in over two months to pick up a shipment? They were too crammed with projects," I told Gina in disbelief at the oversight.
"Great guns, do we have to think of everything," she said shaking her head in disgust.

He remembered this piece of information clearly because someone with an accent called about it recently. He retrieved the email and was furious no one even considered checking it out.

"Their supply of pills must be plentiful."

"Holy samoley! What a horrible development. I wonder what we'll find?" Gina questioned with excitement and anticipation.

Our warehouse number was 1301. Three and one were my lucky numbers, so we pressed ahead. Gina's low cut sweater was a plus. We made a concession on the trench coats but still insisted on wearing our spiked boots in case a need for them arose. I was hoping it wouldn't.

I waggled the location of the key out of Trevor like I planned. Tucked in my boot was my handy small stunner. I grew to adopt Gina's philosophy: One never knows what might happen. She was right. I hoped we wouldn't have to play the bang bang zap game.

She donned light pink boots adorned with sequins and gold, they were totally out of place. But they were quite distracting. That was appropriate for our ruse.

The guard turned around and smiled. She gave him goo goo eyes and batted her lashes. I saw he had the manifests. When his back was turned and distracted by small talk to

Gina, I found the Russian's number. Their company is named 'Troika,' I discovered.

Gina's magic was bliss to hear.

"Thank you. I appreciate your help immensely," I heard her say.

"No problem young lady. Be safe. I hope you get to your appointment on time."

He then settled with a look of lust that was wholly detectable. He paid fervent attention to where she was going, but never noticed me. Our angle worked like a charm.

We commenced toward the warehouse, but were stopped in our tracks.

"Whoa! Where the hell do you ladies think you going?" challenged someone with a Russian accent that I knew all too well.

I remarked, "Tso?" (What)
"Ah, little lady speaks Russky," another one remarked maliciously.

"Ya naz nam, (I don't know)."

"You don't play coy with us. We know who you labor for. We were warned to watch for you," remarked the taller one. "Ivan, what you think we do with these lovely scheming women?"

I failed to believe our reputations had this far a reach.

Ivan replied, "We take hostage, no, Dimi? We have to find out where our drugs be. We must call Kostya, the 'Bull' about this."

In a flash, our hands were tied behind our backs and we were taken to the Russians' warehouse, which stunk of cabbage and beer just like they did. We nearly heaved at the odor.

"Our shop never smelled like this. Oh, mercy," I whispered to my friend. "We must find a way to bottle the scent of cabbage and beer. We wouldn't have to worry about ugly dumb guys bothering us ever again," I remarked sarcastically. "Suddenly grinding meat sounds good."

I blundered when I spat, "Kiss my ass" in Russian.

Dimi grew furious, dragged us to a dark, dank corner in the back, and tied us to a post.

"Apologies, Gina," I said remorsefully. "I can't stand people like that."
"What the hell did you say to the guy anyway?" she seethed.

I hadn't heard that tone of voice come out of her in years.

"I told him to kiss my ass," I admitted.

"Oh, great pyramids of Egypt help this thick head. She wasn't made to be a saint, but she does her best, honest. Why would you do that?" she hissed after she offered up her prayers.

I dropped my head like a juvenile and admitted, "Because I could. Oh crap."

"Oh no, I shouldn't have said that. I aggravated an already horrible dilemma. I got you into all of this. It's my fault, my damn sense of adventure. Our guys and their company have been remiss in finding culprits, so we stick our noses into it once again. Now look where it's gotten us. Some adventure."

The ugly captors checked on us and we stayed silent. We tried our move when their roaming eyes looked elsewhere, and when they were smoking. Ugh, the dastardly smoke odor mixed with the other odor was sickening.

Here we were sitting on a warehouse floor and listening to Ivan say, "I'll make phone call to the 'Bull'". To whom that dubious moniker belonged, we guessed it was the boss, the big kahuna.

"Look, Egypt, you didn't drag me screaming into this. I came seeking answers, too. I wanted this as much as you. So, shut up, already. Let's show the courage we've always had. Remember saving Luigi from those Albanians in Italy? That took guts and courage."

Biting my lower lip, I knew she was right. Still, I was worried. "Sure. Until now, I had courage. This is the Russian mob we're dealing with. Mobs like this can be brutal, especially Russian mobs. It begins with being tied to a pole, and after that, only God knows what." I pressed my hands to my temples to stop the throbbing. "What the hell was I thinking? How could I have come up with this rotten plan in the first place? This is a disaster."
Gina stared at me with that squinty-eyed look that I knew meant she was using anger to cover her fear. I was sure she thought I'd given up. I squared my shoulders and returned her gaze. "Well?"

"Okay, Egypt. Let's stop this crap and evaluate our possibilities—like you taught me. You're the genius here, so stop whining and put that twisted brain of yours in gear. This should be a slam-dunk for you."

"We were ambushed. It happened so fast, I couldn't think." I lowered my voice to a whisper. "Don't glower at me like that. I'm not a miracle-worker."

I regretted the insane decision to uncover the real story about the mix-up with the drugs but didn't say this to Gina. Instead I surveyed our surroundings and sized-up our captors. I knew we had to escape soon. This was no time for fear and hesitation. I had to think, and think fast. Taking a deep breath, I closed my eyes. Images of what happened unfolded to my inner vision. *What, what, what? How do we get out of this?*

After a few minutes, I opened my eyes. My solutions came up as empty as a wino's bottle. *How did I think we were so invincible that we could accomplish anything? What a fool.*

My hands shook and my stomach twisted into knots. I was scared. We both knew that we had to be gone before Kostya arrived. He's not called 'The Bull' for nothing. This could mean painful deaths.

Cogitating began slowly, "Oh, crap, what could the 'Bull' be like?" I blurted out. "A thick neck, tangled, sweaty hair, about 300 pounds, and probably spittle hanging from the corner of his mouth. I'm right about him. I just know it."

"Damn, I'm frightened enough without that description. Stop it," Gina was almost crying.

"Okay, okay, I know. I'm out of my mind with fear too. Sorry, again."

"Oh, quiet with that sorry crap."

Ivan remarked jovially, "I have two lovely snakes in the grass who work for Eternal Treasures." The rest was in Russian and I caught only a tinge of the conversation. It sounded scary. Gina and I exchanged worried glances.

"Our boots, Gina, our boots!" Gina! Something we should have remembered. It was your idea."

"What are you babbling about, Egypt?"

"Our boots, Gina, our boots!" I lowered my voice so the guards couldn't hear. "How stupid can we be? We have to try. How can you forget again?"

Let's get our boots to work," I urged her. "They need some tender looking after I'd say."

"Do you think he's gonna kill us?" Gina whispered. The panic on her face matched mine.

"Perhaps if we appear submissive they might let their guard down while we jiggle and wiggle. Then maybe we could finagle our way out." I avoided her question.

When would we ever learn?

For the time being we focused our attention on getting the damn ropes cut. Gina had her boot knife per usual, but being tied to the post, freeing ourselves was going to be mighty tricky, especially if our captors kept looking back.

"Let's keep the noise down and they won't even care. They're too busy drinking beer and smoking. They await the mighty 'Bull'. You would think he was the pharaoh." I told her that hoping to relieve both our tensions while praying my estimation was correct.

She forced her butt up and tried hard to put her sequined feet up in the air, shaking like crazy. She wiggled in her effort to slide the weapon further down to where I could reach it. From my perspective, she looked like she was doing the air rumba or scratching her ass. Our captors had to keep their backs turned if she was to continue. Time was the chief factor.

"Oh, hell, this is hurting and it's not easy in this mini skirt, which is now giving me a wedgie," she complained.

"Hurry, hurry, shake fast, Gina. Hurt your ass or die, dearie. Pretend there's a scorpion in your boot and shake." We were adamant about escaping.

That's when I dove into my part in the scheme. To be successful we would have to be exceedingly furtive. Gina had the knife and I had the tiny stunner. How I wished at that moment it was a real gun. *Why oh, why do we have to be so damn nosey!*

"If my Uncle Quarto knew what I got myself into…oh, if he only knew. I wish he knew!"

When she heard Ivan approaching us, she ceased her rumba and resumed quietude.

"What you say, lady?" inquired Ivan, his forehead furrowed.

"What do you mean?" Gina questioned, afraid of the implication. "Dear Lord, he heard me mention my uncle," she looked over to me for comfort and consolation.

"Answer the man, Gina," I urged, thinking something unusual was about to be unleashed.

"You do not mean Quarto Scarpetta, no?"

"Oh, so my uncle's credentials run this far? Yes, I mean Quarto Scarpetta."

"So, what's this Quarto business and why you care?" mumbled Dimi.

"Boshe, Boshe (God). I can't believe this."

"Tso? Why you care about her family?" Dimi asked.

"You know Three Fingers Dimitri?" Ivan said with fear.
"Da (yes)," replied Dimi.

"Quarto." Ivan replied.

"He did that? He chop fingers off?"

"Da. And the cripple, Pieter?"

"Quarto?" He showed his fright in a hushed tone as he made the rhetorical inquiry.

"Da. And Boshe (God), Boshe, Ivanso who was dragged out of river. Bless his poor soul."

"No, Quarto again?" shivered Dimi.

With a dejected and worrisome look Ivan replied, "Da. He's all over, like you say, octopus. He has eyes even in the skies."

"This cannot be. It's only a coincidence that it is same name, no?"

"Nyet, cannot be. There is only one Quarto Scarpetta. One does not mess with him. I know it has to be him. How many Quartos can there be. He is BIG boss. I must call 'Bull' and tell him to see what he will say. Maybe good, maybe not." Ivan mumbled to himself about the strange situation as he paced. He summoned the courage and called. After this seemingly never-ending conversation we heard, we began to believe we might have some hope in sight. Perhaps we'll live to see the rays of the sun once again.

While he was yakking, Gina was doing her dance to loosen the knife and it began sliding out.

"Come on Gina, dance your cheeks off."

She looked bedraggled, but she sat down with her weapon sticking out a bit. I tugged one last time and finally got it free. Saving our rejoicing for later, we sat back to back and

170

proceeded in earnest with our escape plan. I hoped it wasn't our last day of screwing up in this world we created for ourselves. The cutting commenced.

Ivan and Dimi stopped ogling us, so I cut and cut. I was slicing my way through when I heard Ivan's cell ring. It was likely this 'Bull' character. Only the tone indicated whether it was good or bad. I'll be damned though, the conversation resonated as both. First I heard good, then bad, several hmmms, and finally a huge da.

Uh, oh, I think we are in trouble. I wouldn't relate that to Gina. She might faint right there and leave me hanging. "Ah, yes, my young ladies, Kostya believes you are perfect hostages for our purpose. At least for now, we call you hostages and not corpses," he laughed in a sinister tone.

His horrid breath was so strong of smoke and cabbage it reached us. *"I hope he doesn't have a wife,"* I muttered under my breath.

"Oh, crap!" I thought the bastard was going to beat on us! Now we have time. Like Gina told me, "Keep your cool, girl." She was becoming the smart calming effect person. I was proud of her. What a great protégé. She kept me in check and cognizant. I had to appear conciliatory and I knew that. For once I felt senseless. It took me but seconds to regain my fortitude.

I settled and he turned his back. Before he did, he sported a huge sneer.

Meanwhile, her own face looked ashen. I turned mine the other way! *It isn't easy for me. I can't admit that to her now. I must consider consequences more, and stop being addle brained next time, if there is another time.*

"The rope's about cut. Now when they're distracted waiting for the others, let's do the 'let's get'em' routine." She asked me nicely not to ruin her boots on this escapade. "Yipes, Gina, come on, your life or your boots?"

"Well, I guess my life, I think. Nooo, of course, my life, 'cuz with you I never know if I'll have another moment to survive and face another situation again. Exciting, I think."

"Don't you know how bad this danger is? How brutal they are?"

Gina looked sorry and anticipated her move. "I was trying not to think about the reality."

"The Russkies are too intrigued with whose coming and what the big boss is going to do with us. Let's scoot around."
"Success!" I rejoiced in a low voice.

"Yea, but now what, genius?" retorted Gina.
"Sing Kumbaya," I stated humbly trying to lighten our dilemma.

Momentarily, we heard a great commotion outside the warehouse door. We seized the opportunity to hunch over and steal toward Ivan and the beast. Without any warning, the door began to rise.

By this time, we weren't far from our captors and the rumbling of the door startled us. We tucked ourselves behind a carton.

Before we knew, the sun was shining in and men of all sizes and appearances formed an endless sea. *It looks like some mobster flick!*

Oh, crap! Gina and I spotted some we knew and some we didn't. Whether we recognized them or not they shared one thing in common. They all looked angry and intense.

"Oh, my holy word. Crap. Look, look who they are. "My God!" I shouted in amazement.

Leading the pack, front and center, were none other than Uncle Quarto, Uncle Max, Trevor, Bruce, and maybe the mob boss. My eyes nearly fell out. By God, it was my grandpa. They then proceeded to hash things out. After a few minutes, the proceedings grew a bit rough. That's when we gave each other a look and took our long-contemplated action. I 'stunned' Ivan while Gina held her knife to Dimi's back. Ivan being immobilized, I bolstered her position with my gun.

"What are all of you doing here? How did you know?" I asked with amazement.

The mob assumed that Ivan and Dimi would be the only people present during the 'hostage' crisis, but Trevor and Bruce called in the troops. Uncle Quarto and the 'Bull' did the same thing. We would never assimilate how and why the unforeseen ones were there. I knew their mouths would be zipped. It would be the exordium of 'don't asks'.

None of the regulars we knew came as a huge surprise to us, but when I saw my uncle and grandpa, I let out a gasp. I could barely muster a word.

"Uncle Max, grandpa, what in the name of all saints are you two doing here?" I grilled.

Grandpa's first response was, "Quarto told me about your dire situation and I knew I had to run and protect you."

"One more time, Uncle Max, what do you have to say? What really brought you here? Even Quarto probably wouldn't get you to New York in time."

"Okay, okay, my little smart ass. We work for Trevor and Bruce too. Well, Pop did one time, and before you go gettin' any ideas, that's all the info you're gonna get from anyone."
"Well, at least you 'fessed up to that much. I love you, all of you. Thanks so much," I gushed, backing down.
"That goes double for me, guys, especially you, Joey and Ricky. And I think that other man must be Angelo, the one Egypt heard you on the phone with on our visit to Mom's, right, Uncle Quarto?"

Quarto commented, "You gals seemed to have a lot of this under control by yourselves, but I'm happy we made it in time before Kostya and his hackies arrived." He moved in to hug Gina. "I like to take things into my own hands so the mission will go our way, my angel," he said.

Gina looked aside at me and spouted, "My uncle knows who Kostya is?"

"Of course he does, remember what happened to these hulk's friends?"

"I'd rather not. I'll pretend I didn't hear that at all. I love my uncle," Gina said in concern and shock.

I made some inane statement to Uncle Quarto that had nothing to do with the situation. He looked at me as if the stress rendered me cuckoo.

"Anything for my crazy, brave girls," he claimed while holding us both around our shaky shoulders. "But I should be punishing you instead." It was an admonition with a slight smile. "Please, next time, let me do the job. Call on Quarto anytime."

The mix-up Crypto caused was adequately remedied when everything culminated that frightening day. The Crypts had transposed warehouse numbers to accomplish their dirty act, changing it from 1301 to 1310, which was the mob's place.

174

Oh, how convenient. Once each other's items had been exchanged, the mob was quite happy. The 'Bull' arrived as the transaction was being completed. He did have a thick neck and skuzzy hair as I said. He gave a big smile of relief and offered his hand to Bruce.

I could see Bruce wipe it on his pants afterwards. He had to view him as pond scum.

They weren't aware that someone might blow the whistle on their warehouse one day. Who knew how far Quarto's capabilities and contacts extended?

"Thank heavens this whole situation is resolved. Problem disappeared," with a deep sigh of relief. "Let's move out, ladies," Bruce told us as he pushed us gently. He didn't look happy. We were scolded with his eyes.

I kept saying to myself, "never again, never again."

"Ah, gently into the sun and freedom," I mouthed to Gina in satisfaction.

She was still quivering a little, but looking down and dusting her boots off in spite of everything. I smiled and shook my finger at her.

***

A few days later, while at work something profound happened.
As if an earthquake rumbled beneath us, the building shook for several seconds. We all looked around, confused a few moments, we bolted. We scurried outside for protection, and to see what happened.

I asked a few passersby. One of them answered, "That puff of smoke looks like it's coming from somewhere down by the docks."

I whispered to Gina, "Oh crap, don't tell me your uncle blew up the mob's warehouse."

"Hell, he wouldn't tell me if he did. But it looks as if it may be his 'brand of law'."

We both began laughing so hard that we had to cover our mouths. *Could this be his handiwork?*

Joey saw us guffawing and inquired, "May I be privy to what you two are muffling your chuckles about?"

Drats! We hoped no one noticed.

"Oh, nothing drastic, really, Joey," answered Gina to her lover. "I hope no one was hurt."

Joey looked at us in a quandary. "I can't figure you two out. I guess I'll have to stop myself from attempting. You two are mysterious ladies."

CHAPTER TWENTY-EIGHT

As I packed for my holy grail of trips—an actual dig in Egypt—I thought carefully about what sort of clothing to take. I wasn't going to be skimping and took clothes for all occasions. Holding up the polka-dot swimsuit, it occurred to me that Egypt was mainly a Muslim country and women didn't wear bikinis. In fact, even the non-Muslim women dress modestly. *Hmmm...* I rolled it up and packed it anyway. Who knows? The hotel might be inclined toward more 'western' ideas of modesty.

Gina came into the room. "This is a chance to follow your dream." She put her hand around my waist and hugged me.

"I know. I'm excited. I'm beyond excited."

"It'll seem odd to go on a trip without you. I mean, I'll enjoy my trip around Europe but it would be better with my best friend." Gina pouted. "And, then there's Joey..."

Joey. Mentioning Joey made me think of Trevor. The thought of leaving him behind tarnished my otherwise bright mood. *He said he would visit. That's something anyway. I just wish he was coming with us. But, he said he had other important roles to play in the U.S.*

"What has Joey told you?" I asked.

"Not much. He has other obligations that he can't ditch. He said he would keep in touch and come to see me when he could. I'm not holding my breath." She turned her face away. I assumed that she didn't want me to see how upset she was.

"Let's talk of happier things? I'm sure both men will stick by their word."

Gina smiled. "Okay."

We chatted about Egypt, Europe, shopping and trivial things that made us laugh. I babbled on about what I had learned about archaeological tools and how to work on a dig. I knew she didn't really care, but loved her for not saying so, and after closing my stuffed suitcases, decided to end on a high note. "Well, my real concern about Egypt is, ta-da, do they have pizza?" I winked. "I actually forgot about it the last time."

"Maybe we'd better have one today," she laughed. "Just in case."

I brushed at my slacks and smoothed back my hair. Gina eyed my luggage. "Sweet mama. You must have ten suitcases. It'll take more than one plane to carry them all!"

I roared with laughter at that image. "Well, maybe we'll have to have everyone else fly in a different plane. I got my lessons from the best."

***

Over a large 'everything' pizza at our favorite place in Little Italy, we talked about my trip and of Eternal Treasures. I jumped at the opportunity to go when Bruce approached me with the idea. He felt that both of us needed a 'time out'. "How did your family take the news that you would be gone for months?" asked Gina.

"They were sad, but I can't help that. They'll adjust. I have to hand it to Uncle Max. He never told the family about his work with E.T." I mulled that over a bit. "I would sure like to know what he does for them and Grandpa, too. I'll never ask him though. Thunder and lightning would fall from the sky and the heavens would rage."

178

"I agree," she shuddered.

"Gina, do you have any idea how much sand we will have to move to uncover this thing? It's monumental."

"Yeah, but you're gonna love it." Gina smiled and picked off a pepperoni from the pizza then popped it into her mouth.

She had resolved her aversion to pizza soon after Italy.

"When you get back, I'll bet you'll be more than ready for a spa day."
"Funny."

"And another thing, have you given thought to the possibility that there won't be any hot fudge sundaes?"

"As a matter of fact, I have. I never had one when we made the last trip."

She held up her wine glass and we toasted to pizza and hot fudge sundaes.

I grew a bit more serious. "Do you believe Trevor and Joey about either of them having important obligations? They were pretty mysterious about it and evaded any questions."

"Yeah, I agree it's a bit odd. But I have no choice but to trust them—so far, anyway."

"You're right," I said, but I still wondered.

Gina's eyes popped wide open. "Heavens, Egypt. I hope you don't run into any curses there."

"Have you been Googling King Tut's Tomb?"
"Uh, maybe just a little. I don't want to see you come home with a pox or teeth growing from your head."

I laughed so hard; wine came out of my nose. "Don't worry. There's no such thing as a tomb curse. It makes for good movies, though, and I do love Boris."

Gina's brow wrinkled. "Boris?"

"Karloff. No? Well, never mind." That's for another day.

***

Although Gina had originally arranged to fly to Egypt with me and head off for Europe a few days after that, she rethought that idea. I would change flights in Paris and she would say goodbye there. We would meet again on the Paris-to-New York flight on the way back. Trekking through hot sand wasn't her kind of fun. Plus, I think she was afraid I'd talk her into doing something dangerous. She might have been right. The camel ride decided it for her. No repeat of such an incident would happen to her. I'd never convince her to do something weird again

During the flight to Paris, I congratulated myself for overcoming my fear of flying. I didn't need her to feed me narcotics just to shut up my whining.
The plane was filled. Thanks to Gina we had first class seats. We made a game of scoping out the other passengers to determine if they were suspicious characters or not and of making up stories about their lives.

One man in particular caught my attention. Something about him looked off. I asked the flight attendant about him but she didn't know who he was.

"Sorry, I can't look up his name on the passenger roster," she told us.

"No. That's okay." I thought he looked like a terrorist or hijacker—turban, beard, coal-black eyes. I even thought I spied a bulge around his waist—not belly fat.

I decided to take a stroll past him. I jumped when he spoke up.

"Thanks, Egypt."

"Anandeep? What a surprise, my old friend. I haven't seen you since University."
"I'm just as surprised to see you," he said. "Since we last met, I became a United States citizen." He smiled, showing perfect white teeth.

We chatted a while about the dig, then I returned to my seat when the flight attendant started serving snacks.

***

With the exception of a short bout of 'pharaoh's revenge,' I was having the time of my life in Egypt. I knew what not to eat but I wasn't strict enough, I guess. I quickly adjusted and was fine after that.

Josef, from Russia and El Badri, an Egyptian native, served as our experts on this venture. There were numerous university students and researchers, too. It seemed though that this dig was 99.9 percent men. There were only two women, and that included me and Sarah, from the University of Southern California. I was so glad to meet her. We hit it off right away.

It was hot and dry, and thank goodness, no mosquitoes. Flies were a problem and other crawlies but I was too enthralled in our project to pay much attention.

One of the men gave me a tip, "Wear long sleeves. You'll save your skin and the flies won't bother you too much."

"Damn! I only packed one long sleeve shirt. The next day, I bought more at the local bazaar. Egyptians love to bargain. I learned quickly how to play the game and came away with several shirts and some other things I hadn't planned on buying, including several hats. They were so inexpensive, I couldn't resist.

The sun beat down on my head like a flame thrower. Hats, sunscreen, and dark glasses were a must. I learned that the wind knocked hats off, so I fastened strings to mine. No one cared that I wasn't dressed like a fashion model.

On a break about a week into the dig, Radi, an Egyptian university student, came and sat with me on a hill.

"Egypt. Tell me about America. I hear so much but I do not know what is truth or not." His big brown eyes pleaded with me.

"That's a hard one, Radi. We are so diverse that even going from the North to the South is like being in a different country. Each part of the U.S is different. The landscape changes drastically, as do the dialects, accents, and many traditions. It's a big country."

"Yes," he said. "I hear there is so much to see, it would take a lifetime to visit them all."

"Maybe not a lifetime, but years, at least." I told him about the Grand Canyon, dense forests, the mountain ranges, volcanoes, regional foods—like grits, oysters, barbeque, and more."

"Wow. I hope to visit one day." He looked into the distance. "But now, they are summoning us back to work."

I stood and brushed off my khaki shorts. "If you do come to America, I hope you visit me and my friend, Gina."

He grinned from ear to ear. "Definitely. *Chokran!*"

"*Salaam*," I said in return. I had been practicing my Arabic with Radi, and pretty proud of my progress.

***

We had been on the project for a month when Trevor called again early in the morning. There's about a seven-hour time difference. When to call is tricky.

"Hi Egypt. How is the dig going?"

"Great. I'm having a wonderful time and have met the most interesting people."

"Mm. Actually, what I really want to know is do you miss me as much as I miss you?"

My heart warmed. "If you miss me so much it hurts, then, yes."

We talked for a long time, flirting, and just basking in each other.

The phone line crackled. "Trevor? Are you still there?"

"Yes. But you're breaking up."

"Egypt doesn't have the most reliable cell reception. Love you."

The line went dead.

A few minutes later, Gina called.

"I'm so glad to hear your voice. I love it here," I said.

"I adore where I am, too. I'm lying on a beach in Santorini, sipping iced Ouzo. Wish you were here."

We chatted for a few minutes then there was a knock on my door.

"Bums, Gina. I have to go. The van is waiting to take us to the dig."

"Okay. Talk to you soon. Love you."

"Love you, too."

***

After three months, I had pretty much mastered my Arabic communication skills, adapted to the food, and learned the routine. Everything was moving along like clockwork. One morning, I was inelegantly squatting over a hole in the ground and gesturing to one of the Arab diggers about a scorpion that was on his shoulder.

"Hi there, beautiful."

I jumped and whirled around, the scorpion completely forgotten. "Trevor!" I ran to him. He wrapped his arms around my waist and swung me around. I wanted to kiss him so much, but knew that publicly displaying affection is not acceptable.

"I have missed you so much. I just arranged for you to have today and tomorrow off. How about spending that time with me?"

"Are you kidding? Nothing would keep me here with an offer like that."

His eyes lit up like fire. "I feel closer to you than ever. Odd, considering we have been on nearly opposite sides of the planet."
I wanted him more than ever—right there. I almost dragged him to my tent but restraint held sway, at least until we got to the hotel.

"I know. I feel the same." Electricity shot through when he touched my cheek. "Let's get out of here." I nearly dragged him to his Jeep. He floored the gas and we headed for the hotel.

Eat my dust, guys. I looked back at the cloud of sand behind us. The men were smiling.

Inside my room, we tore off each other's clothes and made mad, hot, wet, sweaty love.

Afterward, I rolled off of him, panting. "That was magic."

He traced my body with his fingers. "There's more magic to come. I promise."

I think it was three times later that our passion was finally spent enough to think of other things.

"Are you hungry?" he asked.

"You bet."

"Me, too. Have you had Egyptian pizza, yet?"

My eyes widened. "No! They have real pizza? I suppose I haven't given it much thought, strange."

"Of course. Pizza is an international food. Egypt's is quite good."

We showered, dressed, and hailed a cab. Trevor gave the driver directions in Arabic to another hotel in Cairo.

"This is where I always have pizza." He touched his fingers to his lips. "Delicious. You remember pizza night, don't you?" he smirked and winked.

Inside, the restaurant was elegant. White table cloths, gleaming crystal, and polished silver made me think I might have teleported back to New York.

Looking at the menu, I blew a low whistle. "Imagine that, not only pizza, but fried ravioli, too."

"Egypt is an international country. Germans, Italians, and the French all have a history here. Remember, that Napoleon's men discovered the head of the Sphinx rising out of the sand."

"Good point."
We ordered pizza and wine. The wine was only so-so, but the pizza had an incredible taste. It was not all the way Italian because it had a touch of Arabic seasoning. It was still wonderful."

***

The next day, when we weren't making love, we were out shopping. I think we would have given Gina some serious competition. We traveled to some of the lesser known sites and explored the Step Pyramid in Saqqara.

"I wish they had found Imhotep's tomb. He is one of the most brilliant people that has ever lived. Think of it! Physician, architect, vizier, mathematician, priest, speaker; the man even did brain surgery."

"Yes, it would be wonderful. He was quite a man," Trevor uttered.

"Imagine. This is even older than the Pyramid at Giza." I was in reverence.

The last site we visited was the Serapeum, where the Sacred Apis Bulls had been entombed. "Did you know, Trevor, that even as ancient as the sarcophagi are that held the bulls, the catacombs here are even more ancient?"

"No. I didn't know that."

"Uh-huh. No one knows how old these tunnels are or who dug them. The Egyptians simply took advantage of them to create the tombs for their Apis Bulls. The complex hasn't even been fully explored, yet."
He ran his hand along the rough, white wall. "Amazing."
That night, over dinner, he turned serious. "I have to go back tomorrow morning."

A tear formed in the corner of his eye. My heart sank.

That night, we made love with an even stronger passion. I tried not to think about him leaving and savored every second with him.

The next morning, I wanted to go to the airport with him, but he insisted that he couldn't take it and would probably embarrass himself in public.

We said our goodbyes.

When he was gone, the room felt empty and cold. *Pull yourself together, Egypt. He hasn't left you for good.*

I called Sarah. "So, Trevor left this morning. I'll be riding with you to the dig."

"Terrific. I'm just about to leave my room, now. I'll meet you downstairs."

***

The heat was growing more brutal every day. We wouldn't be able to keep up the dig much longer. I was just about to think nothing was going to come of this season's work and we would have to wait for months to come back.

"Voila!" called out one of the university students from France. Everyone rushed over. There in the sand was an almost intact vase and a glass gemstone. It was like winning the lottery.

As two people squatted with paint brushes to extract the vase, I began to scoop away sand with my hands. I barely believed it, another find. I shouted, "I found another piece of pottery!" I held a small funerary jar in my hand. Chipped and a little cracked, I smiled like a kid in a candy store. As others gathered around, I held it up to the sun. "I know it's not quite museum quality, but a fantastic find for me."

My enthusiasm fired up, the sun was forgotten. When I found a carved lapis scarab, I nearly fainted. It wasn't just excitement. In my digging fever, I ignored the first rule of the desert—drink plenty of water! I felt dizzy and sick. As I sank to my knees, all I could think was, *you fool.* Then the world went black.

I woke up in my room. The hotel doctor stood over my bed. "You, Miss, had mild sunstroke. It is important not to let yourself get dehydrated."

My head throbbed. "Oooh. I feel terrible." I could barely move.

Sarah stood next to the doctor. "I'll keep an eye on her, now. Thank you for your time."

The doctor nodded. "Fine. Remember, sips of water only. Otherwise it will come right back up."

Sarah walked him to the door.

I fell asleep.

When I woke up, it was late afternoon, near sunset. I felt much better and noticed that the pitcher of water was almost empty. Next to it was a glass with a straw in it. *How did I drink all that when I was asleep?* Then I recalled Sarah. *She must have helped me sip and I just didn't wake up enough to remember.*

My cell phone rang.

"Gina!" I said with as much enthusiasm as I had strength for.

"Hi. Isn't it about time for your dig thingy to be done?"

"Actually it is. We'll be tearing down and securing the site for a couple of days, and then I'll be on my way home. We found some pottery, a glass cabochon jewel, and I unearthed a large, carved Lapis scarab. A bit cracked, but who cares. It's a treasure."

"A what?"

"Scarab. A beetle."

"Oh. Nice. I did a lot of shopping and sent tons of things to our apartment. Expect lots of presents when you get home."

"Thanks." Although she said all the right things, I detected something in her voice that told me she wasn't completely happy.

"Okay. What is it? I know when you're trying too hard to be cheerful."

"Can't hide anything from you. Don't know why I even tried. I haven't heard from Joey for three weeks and I can't reach him either."

"That's odd. I haven't heard from Trevor either. I'm a bit worried. He doesn't answer his cell and never returned my texts. I hope nothing has happened to them."

I shared the conversation I had with Trevor and suddenly it became clear. "I got the same exact same treatment. Unbelievable!"

Did he tell you about details and use cryptic phrases too?" The answer was yes.

These men were unpredictable.

We were worried, annoyed and beleaguered. Talk about tormenting someone.

"It just can't be, Gina. Not after we waited so long for someone."

"Maybe, they're just on a secret mission?" she said with a hopeful tone in her voice.

"Maybe. We'll find out when we get home. I'll see you when you board the plane at Paris. *Oui?*"

"*Mais oui.* See you soon".

We knew they loved us, but we suspected a cloaking of another magnitude. We were concerned they tucked away another agenda that might be considered too dangerous for us to consider. We tried to be diplomatic and yielded to their wishes and asked no questions, trusting them.

They were smooth as river rocks, and slicker than crap. It was a bad analogy, but correct.

***

On the flight back to New York, Gina and I were both antsy. We hoped that Trevor and Joey would be there to meet us. There was still no communication from them. *I just hope it's a secret mission and not something horrible.*

"That's odd," I said when we landed. "There's no answer at Eternal Treasures."

"Hmm. I wonder what's going on."

CHAPTER TWENTY-NINE

We landed in New York and retrieved our bags, then went through endless security checks. No one was there to meet us. Disappointed and puzzled, we hailed a taxi and gave the driver our address.

Inside our apartment, I threw myself down on the bed. I wanted to do nothing but rest.

A couple of hours later, I woke up. Stumbling into the bathroom I nearly screamed at my reflection. What a ghastly mess. My skin was bronze and none too soft. My hair was not in the best shape either. I pulled myself together as much as I could in anticipation of seeing Trevor—I hoped to see him but still no contact and none in sight.

When I stepped into the living room, Gina was sitting on the sofa, one leg tucked under her. She looked radiant. *Does nothing ever tarnish her elegance?*

She looked up. "Ready to head for the office?"

"Ready as I'll ever be."

On the way there, Gina hit me with a bomb.

"I think I'll take a vacation from shopping. I want to focus on my relationship and my best buddie." She winked at me.

We pulled into the parking garage and walked to the elevator. Punching '3', we exited into the hallway.

"What's going on?" I gasped. Where the hell is Eternal Treasures?" The building was empty and the sign with the company name and logo was gone. Peeking into one of the windows all we saw was a great void, no desks, chairs, pictures—nothing.

We rushed back to the elevator and pushed the down button. When the doors opened, we hurried across the lobby. There was a new security guard. When we asked about Eternal Treasures, he shook his head. "I dunno. Never heard of that company. You sure you're in the right place?"

My mind spun with bazillion possibilities, but none of them made any sense. My heart sank as deep as the Barrier Reef. Both of us were stunned as if we had been stung by a million jelly fish. We were frantic.

"There has to be some logical explanation for this," I said. "However, who will tell us what it is?" Oh, crying Cleopatra, where are our men, and where in blazes is the company?" I started to cry with frustration.

Gina cried with me. "What if they're dead or badly hurt? Joey is everything to me. What do we do? Where do we start?"

I wished I could tell her but my mind turned blank as tears poured down my cheeks. "Okay, Gina, let's get it together. Don't focus on the horrid possibilities. Let's examine everything." I wiped my eyes and took a deep breath. "What to do first?" I'm going to call Uncle Max and ask if he knows anything about this."

Gina seemed to brighten up a bit although she was still pale and trembling. "Good. Then if he offers nothing, I'll buzz Uncle Quarto."

I called Max. No answers. Gina called Quarto. No answers. They wouldn't or couldn't tell us anything. So be it. We set ourselves on a quest to find out what happened.

I vowed that nothing would stop us unless we hit a brick wall and maybe not even then. Sometimes our heads were too thick for even that.

"Maybe H.T.H. can dig up more."

"Well, that's something. However, the alphabet had the last and final word. He told us all he knows. There is zip info on these people. It's as if they were never born. They must live in caves. Oh, mercy, the unborn," I heaved a sigh. "But we can still try again." I made the call.

"I know. It's a fantasy of mine that we'd find them. Even Uncle Quarto couldn't find out if he tried and you know his connections," said Gina.

Boy, don't I.

While we waited, our brains cranked. Gina and I were looking glassy-eyed and tired. We were angry, sad, frustrated, and hopeful all tied into one. We felt abandoned and hurt by the men we trusted—and by the company, too.

Our brainstorming went on into the night. Slowly a picture formed. We remembered vague hints from Trevor and Joey about unusual circumstances—in case anything happened.

Gina pounded her fist onto the sofa. "I wish Joey had never come into my life. This sucks."

"Maybe it's time to give our brains a rest." I yawned. "Let's go to bed and continue this in the morning."

That night, I tossed and turned. Strange dreams swirled in my head. The stars were carrying me to some mountain and depositing me in them. *Mother of Mercy, what the hell does that mean?*
In the morning, I felt slightly better—more like being hit by a car instead of an eighteen wheeler.

Gina looked sadder than ever.

We talked as we swirled our breakfast around the plates. We didn't come up with any more possibilities.

Later that day we ordered Chinese food. All we managed to do was pick at it. We dragged around the apartment like forlorn puppies with no treats. To say we were upset was an understatement. I was so distraught I didn't even want pizza.

"I have an idea," I said as I scrolled through the company employee phone list. "Let's call every one of our contacts."

"Great idea. Someone might have a clue." Gina perked up.

But, after calling everyone on the roster that we had numbers for, and there weren't that many, no one answered phones. In fact, most had been disconnected. We were no closer to a solution.

"Is this a conspiracy?" I mused. "Was this all a big joke on us?" That didn't feel right.

The phone rang.

"H.T.H! What did you find out?" I held my breath and put him on speaker so Gina could hear.

"Geez, Egypt. It's like E.T. and all information about them and Crypto has been wiped from the face of our Earth."

I nearly screamed. If Harry couldn't find anything, there wasn't anything to find.

"Thanks anyway. Let us know if *anything* comes up."

"Will do. You girls okay?"

"Uh, thanks. We're fine," I lied.

After disconnecting, a light bulb went on in my head. "Gina, did you hear him say '*our* Earth'?"

"That's odd," said Gina. "Maybe he just misspoke."

***

For three weeks, Gina and I lived like zombies. There was nowhere left to search. We bribed the security guard to let us into the offices to inspect them. Every nook and cranny had been cleaned.

"Gina, this is really bizarre. Look," I pointed to the corner in the storeroom where the strange door had been. "It's gone."

She ran her hand along the wall. "It looks like it was never there. Huh?"

After leaving, I got the idea to phone the Antonios in Italy. They had no clues either. "What in blazes is going on?"

Gina threw up her hands. "We're being stonewalled. I'm starting to be more angry than sad."

"Me too. Let's get to the bottom of this. I know if we stick together, we can find the answers."

We hashed over what we knew and what we didn't know to find a starting place. We found a bench and sat down to rest for a bit.

"Egypt, let's make a pact to be careful and not go storming in where danger lurks."

"Okay. Let's take it slow and logical. Unlike we usually do. Any ideas? We must begin once again whether we like it or not. They are gone, poof, and we have to start thinking of ourselves again."

She put her finger to her chin and puckered her lips.
"Thinking. I'm thinking."
While she was pondering, an idea came to me. I spoke
fashion to her. "What problems do you have in relation to
your diminutive size and height with clothing?" I had a seed
germinating in my brain.

That set her off. After she finished railing about needing her
clothes altered constantly, a seed of an idea began to grow
in my now fertile mind.

"What was that?" I gripped Gina's arm. "It felt like an up-and-
down ripple flowing over and through me."

"I felt it too. That was too weird."

"Yeah, like a phantasm. That was extremely strange."

I tried to stand up but couldn't. Neither could Gina. We
looked at each other wide-eyed."

"Is it affecting the whole world, or just us?" asked Gina.

"I don't know—"

Another wave flowed around us. Neither of us could speak
but we knew something or someone was watching us."

After a few seconds, the effects wore off and we were fine.

"Whoa!" said Gina. "I know Joey was watching me. I felt
him."

"Me too. Trevor, I mean."
This meant we could relax. Our men were around
somewhere and watching out for us. At least that's what we
chose to believe.

"We're going to see them again, aren't we, Egypt?"

"You bet we will. They must be hiding somewhere for a good reason. They'll come out when it's safe. Yes, we'll see them in the future."

I jumped when the Star Wars theme tone rang on my cell phone. "Gina. It's Grandpa. What could he want? I just spoke with him yesterday—

Gina grabbed at the phone. "Answer it. Answer it! Maybe he has something to tell us!"

Sequel to Women on Fire

I hung up after hearing grandpa speak as Gina kept pulling on my arm, "What did he say? Tell me. Does he have any news about the guys?"

"Man, oh man, the usual. Be patient. You'll get your answers one day. Hell, answers, I want our men back," I remarked all in a huff. "Lord of Lords, give us strength."

"Let's just sit and think," I told her.

The sun was already setting, but the air felt a bit chilled as we sat and looked at one another in dismay. Goose pimples ran up and down my arms like little bugs popping up and down under my skin. The atmosphere hung over us like a sad bird's dying call. I wanted to speak, but as my lips were forming they froze for a moment.

"Well, Egypt, what now? How do we pick ourselves up from this turmoil and go on?"

I stared straight ahead with my eyes going back and forth.

"Gina. You know, I think I hear a voice saying go on to something new, while not giving up our quest to find Trevor and Joey," I said in a far off voice. "We won't allow them to hide from us any longer."

Questioning, Gina said, "We won't? Oh no we won't. There has to be a way to track their movements. Isn't there?"

After a moment I told her, "Probably not. I'm sure they went incognito."

Suddenly the air got a bit colder and without answering her I suggested we go back to our apartment and chew on that thought for a while.

We didn't say much on the way back. Both of us were trying to come up with a reasonable strategy for our lives. The apartment had become its own comfort from our worries. It was cozy and enveloped us like a cocoon. If there was ever a word to describe us it certainly wasn't reasonable but impetuous. This time we needed both of us to have a stroke of realistic genius.

"Let's make some tea," I said as I got the water on and searched for one we both enjoyed.

"Thanks. Maybe it'll warm up our brains so we can think."

Think. Hmmm, we hadn't been thinking very well lately, but we were determined to right at that time. There was no placing our lives in stasis for the men. After all, we don't know how long they'd be gone, or if they'd ever come back. Everyone knows now that we are women of action and won't stay still like a dead fish on the beach. Perhaps we were temporarily 'dead in the water', but I knew we'd find some kind of lifeline to pull us up from the void.

The End

About the Author

Carol was born in Scranton, PA and now lives in Rochester, NY with her husband, Jim. She is a graduate of Keystone College & Kent State University with a psychology degree. She was a former caseworker, and vocational counselor. They have a son, Daryl, plus three cats. She is into old muscle cars, and ancient Egypt. Carol began writing plays at age of eight.

For more information,
carolcares4u@aol.com

Find more books from
Keith Publications, LLC
At
www.keithpublications.com

CPSIA information can be obtained
at www.ICGtesting.com
Printed in the USA
BVOW08s0046070917

493970BV00001B/4/P